BLINDSIDE

BLIND FAITH SERIES, BOOK THREE

N.R. WALKER

BLINDSIDE

Cover Artist: Sara York
Editor: Erika Orrick
Blindside © 2013 N.R. Walker
Third edition: 2018

All Rights Reserved:

Warning

Trademarks:

DEDICATION

For Will...

Blindside

MARK'S STORY

BLIND FAITH 3

CHAPTER ONE

I PICKED up the phone receiver. "Mark Gattison speaking."

Another phone call, another customer, another Friday afternoon when five o'clock couldn't come quick enough. I leaned back in my chair and let my head fall back as I talked the customer through their cabling questions, resisting the urge to groan.

Or throw something at the freakin' clock on the wall.

I managed to get through the phone call without offending anyone when Will stuck his head over my cubicle. He made me smile. "Hey."

He grinned back at me, walked around my side of the wall that divided us, and leaned against my desk. "What are you doing tonight?" he asked. "Any plans?"

"Just the usual, I think," I answered, stretching out.

"Kings?"

"Yeah. You? What's your plan?"

"Oh, I might go out," he said. "Not sure yet."

"You should come to Kings with me," I said, raising my eyebrows at him.

Hartford was reasonably sized city, unfortunately with rather limited gay-friendly bars. King and Queens, or just Kings as it was more commonly known, was one of them. I'd worked with Will for a while, then one weekend I saw him out. He was with a guy, so he didn't exactly need to explain his sexual orientation to me.

I had to, though. That particular night, he saw me with some woman and the next Monday, Will tried to gauge my reaction to the fact I'd seen him snogging some guy. I laughed and told him I had no preference. "I like women," I told him, then I nudged his elbow, "and I like men."

His eyes went wide and he blushed. "Oh..."

"I don't prefer one over the other," I said casually. "Just whatever takes my fancy on the night."

"So, no girlfriend?" he asked. Then he cleared his throat. "Or boyfriend?"

I snorted. "Uh, no. I don't do commitment."

Will had laughed at that, then our boss walked in so we went back to work. And from that day, we've been good friends. Best friends.

Will Parkinson was a great guy. He was cute. He had sandy-colored hair and blue-gray eyes and a grin that made me smile. He was probably one of the few guys I'd ever spent time with that I'd never ended up in bed with.

And since Carter packed up and moved to Boston two years ago, I didn't exactly have a lot of *close* friends. Plenty of people I talked to, met out for drinks, or hooked up with.

But no one who *knew* me.

Not that Will had replaced Carter as my best friend, but well... well, he kind of had.

I looked at him, still leaning against my work desk, poking his finger at the bobblehead Yoda on my desk. "Hey, Will, did you wanna go to that festival thing on Saturday?"

Will looked at me and shrugged. "The foreign film one?"

"Yeah, the one you said you wanted to go to."

He gave me a smile. "Okay. Sure."

"So, will you come out with me tonight?" I asked him again.

He didn't look too keen. "I don't know…"

I jumped up out of my chair and stood in front of him, poking my finger in his cheek trying to get him to smile. "Come on, Will. You know you want to."

He rolled his eyes, but he gave me a half smile. He huffed. "You're not gonna leave me there again, are you?" he asked. "You find some random one-nighter and I end up cabbing it home by myself."

"Nope," I declared. "Tonight, I make it my mission to get you laid."

"Mark…"

"Come on, Will," I whined. "How long has it been?" I didn't give him time to answer. "Too long, that's how long. No gay man should abstain for as long as you have. It's not natural."

"Just because you singlehandedly influence the statistics for gay sex doesn't mean the rest of us need to."

"I don't do it singlehandedly," I told him. "Believe me, it takes more than a few hands," I said, waggling my eyebrows at him. "Anyway, you've been in a bit of a funk lately. It might improve your mood."

"In a bit of a funk?"

"Yeah, not your usual self," I explained. "That sexy smile has been missing lately."

"Has it?" he said flatly.

"Yeah, Will. Wanna tell me what's up?" I asked. But then the phone on my desk rang. I stepped away from

Will and picked up the receiver. "Mark Gattison speaking."

"Is that your 'I'm a grown up' voice?" the voice said. "Or your 'The boss is here, I need to *act* grown up' voice?"

I recognized who was speaking. "Isaac?"

"Yes, it's me," he answered. "Carter wanted me to give you a call at work. Hope you don't mind."

"No, I don't mind," I said, smiling at Will, who was watching me. "What can I do for you, sexy?"

"And there's the Mark I know."

I laughed. "No, seriously."

"What's serious?" he asked. "What you can do for me, or that I'm sexy."

"Oh, you're completely sexy," I replied with a laugh. Will rolled his eyes and walked back to his desk.

"Carter wanted me to let you know that we're coming up to Hartford next weekend."

"For real?"

"Yes, for real," Isaac said. "I am supposed to tell you before you make plans."

"I would totally break plans for you," I said.

"You're such a flirt," Isaac said. "Carter will call you later."

"Okay, I'll look forward to it. See you soon."

I hung up the phone and looked over my cubicle wall. "Guess what?"

Will smiled and shook his head. "You're breaking plans with me for some sexy person you're excited to see."

"No, you're still going out with me tonight, and I'm suffering through the foreign film festival for you tomorrow," I said, rolling my eyes at him. "The exciting news is that Carter and Isaac are coming here next weekend!"

"What for?"

"Don't know, didn't ask," I said. "You have to meet them."

"Oh."

"Yeah, it'll be fun. They're really cool."

"So, we're still going out tonight?"

"Yep, you can't get out of it that easy."

"Nothing with you is easy," Will said. Then he looked up from his keyboard. "Except for you."

I gasped loudly. "I'm not easy," I said, defending myself. "I'm just not exactly difficult to please."

Will laughed, then gave a nod to the clock on the wall. "It's home time," he told me. I logged off my computer and tidied my desk, but Will was done before me. "I'll see you there," he said as he was walking out of the office.

"Don't want me to call past in a cab and pick you up?"

He shook his head. "Nah, it'll be okay."

"You're not gonna stand me up, are you?"

Will smiled at that. "Wouldn't dream of it. See you at nine."

True to his word, he arrived at nine o'clock. In he walked, dressed in black jeans and white t-shirt, his short blond hair styled. He looked great. He smiled when he saw me, his teeth matching the brightness of his shirt. I'd already had a few beers by the time he got there and was feeling kinda buzzed.

I handed him a beer and leaned in close so he could hear me. "Hey, stranger."

"Been here long?" he asked in my ear.

"Few beers," I answered, as though that was some universally recognized timeframe. He understood, because he nodded. We were standing so close I got a whiff of his cologne. "You look hot, and you smell great," I told him. I pulled back so he could see my face, and I waggled my eyebrows. "Now let's see if I can get you laid."

He shook his head, took a mouthful of beer, and looked out over the crowd, which I took as my cue. I stood in behind him, so we both faced the crowd, and rested my chin on his shoulder so he could hear me. "What about him?" I said, pointing my beer at some guy. "The guy in the black shirt."

Will shook his head a little, so I moved onto the next guy, then the next and the one after that. But he wasn't interested in any of them, so I suggested another beer and a dance and he loosened up a bit after that.

People quite often confused us for being a couple, or being fuck-buddies at least. We were close. We drank together, we danced together, sometimes we left together. But that was all.

I'd learned a lesson with Carter. Best friends don't fuck. Sure, couples who became best friends did, but not the platonic kind. I'd had plenty of friendships take a nose dive after we'd had sex because things got complicated.

And I didn't do complicated.

Plus, I valued Will too much to lose him. So it was a line we'd agreed to never cross. I remember telling some guy about six months ago at the bar, that no, Will and I weren't together. "We was like peas and carrots," I'd said, giving my best Forrest Gump impersonation, and Will had busted up laughing. He claimed he was the carrot and I was the peas, so I'd assumed we were good.

That's how things were between us.

Even though Will wasn't interested in going home with anyone, I was true to my word. As he'd requested, I didn't leave him to find his own way home. I was all too happy to leave when Will wanted to go.

I even enjoyed the film festival. Not my first choice on how to spend a Saturday evening, but Will wanted to go, so I went along to keep him company.

One French and one Spanish film later, we grabbed some dinner at a local café near the theater.

"The Spanish one wasn't too bad," I told him. "Better than the first one."

"Oh, please," he said, putting his burger down. "What you mean is that the guy in the Spanish film was hotter."

"Well, there was that," I admitted with a grin. "Penelope Cruz is hot, too."

Will had never really acknowledged that I liked girls. Not that he was against it, he just didn't talk about it. He just rolled his eyes and took a mouthful of his burger, chewing thoughtfully.

"You know what you need?" I asked.

He looked up at me, with a mixture of curiosity and fear on his face. "What's that?"

"A boyfriend."

"A what?"

"A boyfriend," I repeated. "Someone permanent. Someone who can go to movies and flea markets and all that shit."

"Don't you want to come with me anymore?" he asked.

"Will, I would go anywhere with you," I told him seriously.

His brow kind of creased, as though he didn't understand. "But?"

"But, I think that's why you're not interested in hooking up with anyone," I told him. "Because you don't do random one-nighters any more. You want someone to hang out with."

He swallowed his mouthful of food and took a sip of his soda. "I hang out with you."

"You want someone to have a relationship with. You know, hearts, flowers, snuggles on the sofa, monogamy, that kind of thing," I explained. "Concepts I don't exactly see the benefits of, to be honest, but a lot of people do. Apparently."

Will chuckled. "It's like a different language to you, isn't it?"

I put my hand to my ear. "I'm sorry, I only speak English."

Will pushed his plate over to me, knowing I'd finish his fries. I always did. "I don't know what I want," he said quietly.

"You want me to find you some hot and hung guy," I declared. "He needs to have the Mark-approved stamp before I let him near you, though."

Will smiled. "Is there a guy left in Hartford that you haven't had some kind of sexual experience with?"

"Is that a prerequisite?" I asked seriously. "Because that's gonna narrow the list down. A lot."

Will laughed at me. "I know it narrows it down *a lot*, but yes, that's a prerequisite. I can't be with a guy if you've seen his dick."

I sat back in my seat and groaned. "Now you're making it tough." I shook my head at him. "I don't know why you don't have guys hanging off you. You're hot, you have a fabulous best friend, and you're packing over eight inches."

Will stared at me.

"I've seen your dick," I told him as I finished his fries.

Will laughed again, and then sighed. "Maybe it's because everyone who's half decent thinks we're together?" he said it as though it was a question.

"Then we should try going to different places," I suggested. "Still together though, you and me. Just to different bars." Then I added, "And your date. And if I bring a date too..."

"*You* bring a *date*?"

"Yeah, I do dates," I said, flicking my straw from my soda at him. "Anyway, next weekend when Carter and Isaac get here, we should go out somewhere nice. I'll find a date for you, and we'll go somewhere that's not a bar or a club."

He reluctantly agreed. "Ugh. Okay, but remember, no one you've been with."

Now seriously, how hard could that be?

CHAPTER TWO

APPARENTLY, it was rather fucking hard. I mean, there were still a lot of guys in Hartford whose dicks I hadn't seen, but thinking any of them were worthy of William Parkinson was the difficult part.

I wanted the best for him. This wasn't for some random one-night stand. This was looking for boyfriend material, and that was a different set of criteria all together.

They had to be worthy.

By the time Friday night came around, and after we'd ordered in pizza, Will was sitting on my sofa going through the short list of possibly suitable guys.

"You can't be serious," he said. "What makes you think you have any say in who I date?"

"Well," I answered from the kitchen. "I'm not letting my best friend go out with just anyone."

"And if I happen to like a guy, but you don't?"

"See, that's why I'm picking him," I explained. "I know what you like. The guy has to work, love Italian food and foreign films. God, I've even factored in your crap taste in music."

"Yeah, thanks," he mumbled.

"I've got a list of guys for you, in no particular order. I asked around, a friend of a friend kind of thing. The first two on the list are friends of my cousin," I told him.

"You're unbelievable," he replied, as though me being unbelievable was an insult.

"I know, right? What would you do without me?"

Will sighed. "I'm not that desperate, you know. I don't really need you to find me someone."

I finished clearing up the dirty plates and walked out to the living room. I sat down beside him. "I just want you to be happy, Will."

"I am," he said quietly. "I just..."

"You're not that happy, are you?" I asked. "Is it being back here? In Hartford? It's been a year."

Will shrugged, but before he could say anything else, the doorbell intercom buzzed.

I patted my hand on his knee, walked to the intercom, and pressed the button that released the door downstairs. I heard footsteps and, knowing who would be standing on the other side, before I opened it I said, "You can only come in if you're both gorgeous."

Carter's voice answered. "Just open the door, Mark."

I pulled open the door and grinned as soon as I saw them. "Hey!" I hugged Carter first, like always. It had been six months since I'd seen him. "Oh my God, I've missed you," I said.

He was holding an overnight bag, so the hug was kind of awkward, but then I let go of him to hug Isaac. I took his hand and led him inside, knowing Carter would follow. "Come in." When we got to the living room, Will was standing up in front of the sofa. "I'd like you to meet my best friend. Isaac Brannigan, this is Will Parkinson," I said, introducing them. "And this is Brady the wonder dog and, of course, my ex-best-friend-because-he-left-me, Carter Reece."

I'd told Will all about Carter and Isaac and about Isaac being blind, and he took the introduction really well. He shook Isaac's hand and then Carter's. "You're the two I've been hearing all about."

"All good, I hope," Isaac said with a smile.

"Of course," Will answered.

I gave Carter another hug. "It's so good to have you here," I told him. "I've missed you. Both of you," I said, including Isaac.

"I hope we didn't interrupt anything..." Carter trailed off suggestively, looking between me and Will.

"Oh, Will should be so lucky," I told them with a laugh. "I was just actually trying to sort out his potential boyfriend list."

Will sighed loudly. "Mark seems to think I need boyfriend and that he needs to be the one to choose the lucky guy."

"Well, he needs to be good enough," I said, defending myself.

Will smiled at Carter. "It's not embarrassing at all."

Carter laughed and put his arm around my shoulder. "Sounds like nothing's changed."

Still staring at Carter, Will asked, "Was he like this with you?"

"All the time."

"Hey now," I interrupted them. "You two are supposed to just get along, not gang up on me." I left Carter and walked over to Isaac, sliding my arm around him and nuzzling his neck. "They're picking on me already."

Isaac laughed. "You just wanted to smell me, didn't you?"

"Absolutely," I admitted without shame. "You always smell so good."

"Mark," Carter warned. "Hands."

I pulled away from hugging Isaac and slid my arm around his waist instead. "How was your trip, guys?" I asked. "Sit down and tell me, what was the point of this little trip back to ye olde Hartford?"

Then Carter said, "Isaac, should I tell him or show him?"

"Show me what?" I asked excitedly.

"You go sit down," Carter said. "I'll grab it. It's in our bag."

I led Isaac and Brady to the sofa. As we sat down, I asked, "How did Brady travel?"

"Oh, he was fine. Slept most of the way," Isaac said. "We only had to stop once so he didn't pee in the Jeep."

I smiled and squeezed his hand. "You look really good, Isaac," I told him. "You look happy."

"I am," he said simply.

"And Carter's so in love it makes me nauseous," I added, smiling at my friend as he walked back toward us.

Isaac laughed, and when Carter sat down, he was grinning. "Here, Mark. This is for you."

I took the thick envelope, and dropping Isaac's hand, I opened it. I pulled out the black and white thick paper. It was folded, and when I opened it to read it, I saw it was an invitation.

Carter and Isaac's wedding invitation.

It was folded like a book. On one side was handwriting, on the other was Braille. *Carter Reece and Isaac Brannigan would be honored...*

I threw myself at Carter, hugging him. "Oh my God. That's so great!" I told him. I was surprised by how emotional I got. I mean, I knew they were getting married. I was there when Isaac proposed—I helped him buy the rings, for God's sake—and they'd talked about and had been planning bits and pieces, so I shouldn't have been so surprised. "It's wonderful," I said again.

It was then I noticed Will looking at me a little oddly, probably wondering what on earth was going on. I handed him the invitation and sat myself back next to Isaac.

"We wanted to hand deliver yours," Carter said. "Plus I wanted to show Isaac around Hartford. You know…"

"Because all things from Hartford are awesome," I finished for him.

Isaac laughed. "Yeah, so Carter keeps saying."

"It's true," I said. "Isn't it, Will?"

Will didn't answer me, so I looked at him in time to see as he ran his finger over the Braille side of the invitation. When he looked up, he looked straight at me.

"It's pretty cool, huh?" I asked.

He nodded. "It's incredible."

Carter smiled proudly. He really did look very happy. "You knew we'd talked about the date, but it's now official. You have two months to rent a tux."

"And I'm still not Best Man?" I asked with a sniff.

Carter had told me earlier, it was nothing personal, but he wouldn't need me to stand beside him in the ceremony. He and Isaac had decided they'd walk down the aisle together, stand together, and walk out together. With Brady, of course.

"No, Mark," Carter said with a resigned sigh. "Your awesomeness will be required to attend and be handsome, but that's all."

"Well, that's a given," I said. Will stood up, and on his way to the kitchen, he handed me the invite. As soon as I saw it, I caught something I hadn't noticed before. Not just my name, but what was written after it.

I looked back at Carter and Isaac. "What do you mean 'Mark Gattison *and friend*'?"

"Well, it was nicer than writing 'plus one'," Isaac said.

"Or 'regular fuck'," Carter added.

Isaac hissed at Carter, presumably for the language. But I didn't care about that. "A *date?*" I asked incredulously.

"Yes, Mark," Carter said slowly. "Someone you've probably been out with more than once."

Will snorted from the kitchen. "Good luck with that."

I glared at him, then had a great idea. "You!"

"Me, what?" Will asked.

"You'll be my date!"

"I'll what?" he asked again.

"You can come with me," I told him. "To Boston. To the wedding."

"As your date?"

"You don't have to put out or anything," I told him. "I'm sure we won't be the only four guys there that do guys."

Will rolled his eyes, then looked at Carter. "See what I have to put up with?"

"Better you than me," he replied. "I did my time in your shoes."

I sighed dramatically. "Isaac, they're picking on me again."

Will came back with drinks for everyone, putting three beers on the coffee table, but he put one in Isaac's hand. "Can I get you guys something to eat?" Will asked. "Mark here forgot his manners."

"No, I didn't," I argued with Will. "Carter's like you. He helps himself in my house."

Will ignored me. "There's fresh pizza we ordered tonight. I can heat that for you if you want?"

"No, we're fine," Carter said with a smile. "We grabbed something on the way. Thank you anyway, Will."

"Thought someone here should be a good host," he said, sitting back in the sofa and taking a mouthful of beer.

"Is it the International Pick on Mark Gattison Day today?" I asked. "Because I missed the memo."

"Only important people got it," Will said without missing a beat. "Actually, I think it was classified."

I looked at Carter and sighed. "See what I have to put up with?"

Isaac laughed. "Are you sure there's nothing more between you two?" he asked. "You sound like you're married."

"No, Will here has the prestigious honor of being my friend," I said. "Actually, Will's the closest thing I have to a best friend since Carter here decided to leave me and fall in love."

"Who the hell else could put up with you?" Will said with a smile. "There's not room for anyone else in your life besides you and your ego."

I pouted. "Aw, Will, don't be like that. I might start to think you don't love me."

Isaac snorted. "And what's not to love?"

"Exactly!" I said, taking a mouthful of my beer. "That's what I keep telling him."

Carter put his feet up on my coffee table and swigged his beer. "Will, tell me about you. How did you have the misfortune of meeting Mark?"

"We work together," Will answered.

I elaborated. "We share a cubicle wall."

"How is the world of cable engineering?" Carter asked.

"Absolutely riveting," Will answered flatly.

"Busy," I added. "Same shit, different day." When I'd gone to university to study engineering, it wasn't exactly where I saw myself headed. But, it paid the bills and then some, and in this city that was a blessing. "How's school, Isaac?"

"Great," he answered. "I love it."

"Tell me, how're Hannah and Carlos doing?" I asked. "And that gorgeous little Ada?"

"She's walking now," Carter said with a grin. "She's a cheeky thing. Full of mischief. She's such a Brannigan."

Isaac chuckled. "They're all fine. Hannah said to say hi."

"And Brady?" I asked. The dog's ears picked up and his tongue lolled out the side of his mouth.

Isaac's free hand automatically went to the dog's head, scratching him softly. "He's great," he said. "Don't know where I'd be without him." Then Isaac tilted his head. "Literally. No clue where I'd be."

I laughed. "Oh my God, Isaac. Did you just make a blind joke?"

Will narrowed his eyes at me, as though I shouldn't say such things. But Carter shook his head with a smile. Looking at Will, he pointed between me and Isaac. "These two are trouble when you put them together."

I stood up and asked Isaac for his hand.

"What for?" he asked, but held up his hand anyway.

"We're going to dance," I told him. "Like we always do."

I pulled him to his feet and led us to a more open space near the kitchen. When I pulled him against me and slid my arm around his back, he said, "You just wanted to smell me again, didn't you."

"Shh," I hushed him, loud enough for Carter to hear. "Or Carter will be on to us."

"Just keep your hands above the belt, Gattison," Carter warned.

Will finished his beer. "Well, it's been a pleasure," he said. "But I'll let you guys have some catch-up time."

I stopped moving my feet. "Will, don't go. You can stay."

"No, it's okay," he said, getting to the front door. "I'm tired, and I'll see you all in the morning anyway." Then he looked at Carter. "God knows what he has planned for us."

Carter quickly got to his feet. "I'll walk down with you," he told Will. "Isaac, I'll just take Brady down for a pee before it gets too late."

"Okay," Isaac answered from my arms. When the door closed behind them, Isaac just kept moving his feet, slowly dancing. "So, Will seems like a nice guy."

"He's great," I agreed. "Puts up with my shit, anyway." Isaac was quiet for a second, though he never stopped dancing. "You and Carter seem happy. Well, I can tell you Carter certainly does. He hasn't stopped smiling since he got here."

Isaac stopped moving then. "He is. So am I." Then he sighed, "I'll admit, when he first wanted us to go to counseling together, I just did it to make him happy. He wanted it, and I'd been so horrible to him I would have done anything to make it up to him..."

"But?"

"But it really was the best thing," he said quietly. "For me, for us. We talk more, about everything. I think I can safely say I'm the luckiest man on the planet because I have him."

"He is kinda cool," I admitted with a smile, knowing Isaac would hear it in my tone. "Don't tell him I said that."

Isaac laughed. "I'm totally telling on you."

I pulled him against me and started to dance again. "Oh, so that's how it's going to be? You're on his side now."

"Completely," Isaac said, almost dreamily.

While we were talking about mushy stuff, I said, "And the big wedding, huh?"

Isaac smiled at the mention of it. "I can't wait."

"Oh God," I said with a groan. "You've become one of those sappy, I'm-so-in-love kind of people."

He sighed loudly. "Yeah, it's disgraceful, isn't it?"

"Utterly appalling."

Isaac kept on slow dancing, though he never lowered his hands to my ass, which was quite disappointing. "I never thought I'd have *that*, with anyone," he said. "Let alone with someone like Carter."

"Have what?"

"That kind of love," he said simply. "It's just so... absolute. You know that warmth in your chest, that *knowing*, that you've found the one."

I stopped dancing and pulled back a bit so I could see his face. "Well, no... I don't know what that's like."

Isaac tilted his head. "You've never been in love?"

"Every Friday and Saturday night," I told him. "For about half an hour."

Isaac smiled, just as Carter and Brady came back inside. Carter was mumbling about the cold when he stopped and looked at us. "Still dancing?"

"If that's what you'd call it," I said. "I think Isaac just wanted to feel my ass."

Isaac pushed me on the shoulder. "I did not."

Carter laughed and as he unclipped Brady, I said to him, "Come on, Car. Your man here needs you. I told him my ass is not his to feel."

I stepped away and Carter took my place. He slipped his arms around Isaac, and Isaac all but melted into him with a quiet sigh.

It was very different to how I'd just danced with him. They held onto each other, like really held on with their hands almost gripping each other, as though they were holding on for dear life.

I fell back onto the sofa, picked up my beer, and took a mouthful.

Had I ever known love like that?

No.

Did I *want* to know love like that?

No.

I didn't. I didn't want to depend on someone else like that. I didn't want to trust anyone else; I didn't want to lose any part of myself.

I took another mouthful of beer, draining the bottle, and convinced myself I didn't need what they had. I didn't need love absolute, as Isaac had called it. I didn't need the love of someone else to validate myself.

I didn't want the complication. I didn't want the inevitable breakup and the subsequent heartache. I picked up Will's abandoned half-empty beer and took a mouthful of it. I just needed casual sex with strangers. That's all I'd ever need, I thought to myself as I finished Will's beer and watched Carter and Isaac slow dance in my living room.

CHAPTER THREE

WILL ARRIVED at my apartment midmorning wearing jeans and a new jacket I'd not seen him wear before. He'd barely done the rounds of conversation with Carter and Isaac before I was ushering us out for coffee. The beauty of living in an apartment in the city center is having everything within walking distance.

We walked past a much-closer Starbucks but made our way to my favorite café for coffee. It was a rule of mine never to frequent commercialized, franchised coffee shops when smaller, independent cafés still existed. Carter and Will were very well-versed in this conversation with me, and when Isaac questioned why we walked past two perfectly good coffee houses, they both groaned.

"Because Mark hates franchised cafés," Will said with a sigh.

"And we're not allowed to go in them," Carter added.

I think Isaac was waiting for a punch line. Instead, I told him, "It's my one pet peeve. I'm rather passionate about it."

"And by passionate," Will said, "he means stubborn and ranty." They all laughed at me.

"Laugh at me all you want, but I'm a man of principle."

Will held the door open of the much smaller, more personalized coffee shop. "You're a man of many things. I'm not sure principle is one of them."

I gave him my best death-stare as I walked in, but I promptly asked for a table for four. We sat down and ordered coffee and food.

Will was all smiles with dimples, and when I asked him the reason for his good mood, his smile grew even bigger. "Well, I might have called that guy on the list you gave me yesterday."

I almost dropped my coffee. "Which one?"

"The first guy on the list."

I rolled my eyes. "Tim? Jim? Jack? What was his name?"

"Jayden," Will answered.

"And?"

"And what?" he said with a smile.

"Don't act coy with me, Will Parkinson," I tried using my stern voice. "Spill the details. Is he coming for dinner tonight?"

"No way."

"What do you mean 'no way'?" I asked.

Will looked at Isaac and Carter, who were kind of caught in the crossfire. He apologized to them, then lowered his voice to speak to me. "There's no way I'd bring someone to meet you on the first date. You'd scare anyone."

"But I introduced you!" I cried. "Well, kind of."

"I'll meet him first," Will said, "and if he's worthy of a second or third date, then you can meet him."

"A third date? I need to meet him before a third date!" I looked at my oldest friend. "Carter, back me up!"

"I'm with Will on this one," he said calmly.

I put down my coffee. "I'm beginning to regret letting you two meet. You're both supposed to be in my corner, not ganging up against me. You know, like, if I'm Batman, you two will be Robin and Alfred. And believe me, Robin and Alfred would never gang up on Batman."

"Alfred?" Carter asked. "Seriously?"

"Don't underestimate the old guy," I told him seriously. "He kept the best secrets."

"Well, I don't know about being Alfred," Carter said, smiling into his coffee. "But I will always be in your corner, Mark. The last thing Will needs, though, is for you to intimidate any potential boyfriend."

"I don't intimidate anyone," I said seriously.

Will and Carter both scoffed, and then Carter said, "You don't mean to, but your confidence is daunting sometimes."

"What does that even mean?" I asked.

Will patted my hand. "Your awesomeness is too much for some people."

I squeezed Will's hand. "Thanks." Then I looked at Carter. "Why couldn't you say it like that? Alfred would know how to say it."

"Maybe I'm Robin," Carter said.

"Pfft. You are no such thing," I said flatly. "Will is my Robin."

Will grinned, the full double-dimple kind. "I'd be your Robin," he said. "But I draw a line at the tights and green Speedos."

"But that's the best part of his outfit," I said seriously.

"No, the best part of his outfit is his cape," Will said adamantly. "But his is yellow."

"That doesn't matter," I replied matter-of-factly. "It's a cape. The color of the cape is irrelevant."

"Irrelevant?" he repeated. "It is no such thing. It's the *most* important part!"

"I thought you said the tights and underpants were the most important part?"

"Oh my God," Isaac mumbled. "Is this conversation even happening?"

"This is nothing," Will said, taking a bite of his bagel. "Once we debated the pros and cons of eighties music. It lasted for two days."

"I was arguing against," I told them. "He was arguing for."

"You were arguing for the sake of arguing," Will replied. "No one is *that* passionate about teased hair, acid-washed denim and Lycra."

I gasped, and Carter laughed.

"It's true," Will said. "He argues about everything."

"I don't argue," I told them. "I just have opinions."

"On everything," Carter said.

"Isaac, sweetie," I said, ignoring the two traitors at the table. "Looks like it's you, me, and the wonder dog today. These two don't play fair."

"Oh, you love us," Carter said.

"I'm reconsidering my options," I told them.

Will pushed his plate with his half-eaten bagel on it toward me and changed the subject. "Care to tell us what we're doing today?"

"Well, it's Open Studio Day," I told them, picking up Will's leftover bagel and taking a bite. "I thought we could go..."

"What's that?" Will asked.

"It's Oak Hill's art center's exhibition day," I explained, talking with my mouth full.

Isaac's face turned to mine. He was almost smiling. "Oak Hill? Really?"

"Yeah, it might not be that exciting, but I only had a week to find something for us all to do," I said, trying to play it down. "You might be sick of that kind of thing, Isaac, I wasn't sure if you'd be interested but it's their art exhibition day. They even have art classes, or so the website said."

"I would love it," he said, giving me a full smile.

"Um," Carter started, but Isaac cut him off.

"Oak Hill is the name of the Connecticut Institute for the Blind," Isaac said. "I've heard a lot about it, but never been."

"Well, good," I said. "Today you shall go. Then tonight, if you're interested, there's a jazz thing on at The Stage. Normally they do theater but this is some concert. I got us tickets anyway."

Carter grinned at me. "And you want people to think you're cold hearted."

"Shh," I hushed him. "Don't ruin my reputation. I can't have people thinking I'm all kind and considerate. It'd be years of being an asshole down the tubes."

Isaac smiled then. "Your secret's safe with us."

I looked at Will, and he was smiling at me too. "You're not an asshole, Mark."

"Shh," I repeated. "I said keep it a secret! Jeez, Boy Wonder, your secret-keeping skills are sorely lacking. I might have to revoke your cape privilege and give it to Alfred over here."

Will just grinned at me, no sarcastic comeback or anything. Then he said, "What are our plans for tonight? And please don't tell me it involves taking body shots from those Brazilian twins before or after the jazz show."

I burst out laughing. "No... but now you mention it..."

"Who are we taking body shots from?" Isaac asked, a little too keenly.

Carter cleared his throat. "Uh, no one."

"Oh come on, Alfred," I said to Carter. "Where's your sense of adventure?"

"I'd rather my fiancé not drink alcohol from the navels of strangers, thanks anyway," he replied.

I looked at Will. "See what happens when you get married? Do you solemnly swear to never have fun again? I do. Do you hereby swear to never have sex with anyone else, ever again? I do. Do you declare to lose all sense of humor? I do."

Will laughed, Carter rolled his eyes, and Isaac tilted his head. "Mark, where do you get this aversion to marriage from?"

Carter's eyes shot to Will's and they both grinned, slowly. They spoke in unison. "His mother."

"Don't speak of the devil," I warned them. "Jesus, now she'll freakin' call. If my phone rings in the next ten minutes"—I looked at Will, then at Carter—"one of you two are answering it."

They both laughed, of course, as though it was remotely funny. Which it wasn't. At all.

Isaac looked like he didn't know what to say, so I explained, "My mother is... well, she's... not exactly what you'd call maternal."

"She's great," Will said, with a nudge to my elbow.

"Oh yeah, she's a real hoot," I added sarcastically.

Then, because the universe hates me, my phone rang. I fished it out of my pocket and slid it across the table to Carter. I didn't even have to look at the screen. "You answer it. Tell her I'm busy."

Carter laughed and snatched up the phone. "Carter Reece speaking."

I could hear the excitement in the shrill tone of my mother's voice through the phone when she heard Carter. I took Isaac's hand. "It's okay, she may be Satan, but her powers for evil are rendered useless through a telephone. She can't hurt him."

"Satan?" Isaac asked.

I nodded. "Yes, she has evil powers. If you speak her name, the phone rings and it's her."

Will laughed. "Oh come on, she's not that bad."

"Not that bad?" I asked. "When I was sixteen, I'd told her I was going to the movies with some friends, and she told me to go to the cinemas on New Park Avenue because the seats were roomier," I told him. "'Better for giving head,' she said. Those were her exact words."

Will burst out laughing. "Your mom cracks me up."

Isaac's mouth fell open. "Really? She said that?"

"Yep," I said. "I told mom I was taking a girl and she sipped her wine—" I mimicked the action of holding a glass of wine. "—and then she said, 'giving head, getting head, you'll need the same space'."

Carter put his hand over the phone. "Your mom said to stop talking about her."

Ignoring him, I rolled my eyes and looked at Will instead. "I did get five tickets for tonight, so if you want to call your date and ask him to come along..."

Will looked at me for a long moment, but before he could say anything, Carter held the phone out. "Will. It's for you."

Will took the phone and Carter slid his arm around Isaac and grinned. He looked at me. "Mark, your mom hasn't changed one bit."

"I know," I agreed. "Plastic surgery and Botox will do that."

Carter laughed. "I meant personality-wise."

I nodded. "Yeah, that's because she's pickled from the inside out. Wine and gin will do that."

Carter chuckled, but then he leaned in to Isaac and whispered, "She's not that bad."

Will said goodbye to my mother and handed me the phone. I looked at the dark screen. "She didn't want to speak to me?"

He was trying not to smile. "No, she said no need..."

I glared at him. "Will..."

He grinned then. "She said it was nice of you to ask her around for dinner next weekend."

My mouth fell open. "You *didn't*!"

Will put his hand to his chest. "I didn't, no."

Carter laughed. "I did."

I glared at him instead. "Some friend you turned out to be."

My phone rang in my hand and the caller ID told me it was my mother. "I told you," I growled at Carter and answered the call. "Mom!"

"Yes, hello darling," she replied. "Just thought I'd let you know I'll be there at seven. Did you want me to bring anything?"

"No, Mom, it's fine," I said, kicking Carter under the table.

"Okay, darling," she said musically. "You're such a sweet boy. Don't know why some nice boy hasn't snatched you up yet."

And there it was. I let my head fall forward so my forehead rest on the table. "Bye, Mom."

I clicked off the call, and when I looked up, Carter and

Will were grinning. "Come on, Isaac," I said. "These two are being assholes. Looks like it's just you and me."

I stood up, slid my hand over Isaac's, and said, "How about we make our way to Oak Hill, huh?"

Isaac stood up, as did Brady, and we walked toward the door. As we passed the waitress, I looked back and pointed at Carter and Will—who were still grinning—and said, "Those two are paying the bill."

Carter laughed, but I still led Isaac and Brady outside. "We're not really going without them, are we?" Isaac said quietly.

"Nah, they'll catch up," I told him. I linked arms with Isaac, putting my hand on his forearm. I looked behind us, and sure enough, Will and Carter were following. "We have to wait for them at the bus stop anyway."

By the time we walked to the bus shelter, they were right behind us. Carter spoke first, I realized, probably so he didn't startle Isaac. "Your mom said she hopes you cook that Hungarian lamb dish when she visits on Saturday. She said it was good."

"It's not good," I corrected him. "It's awesome."

Will looked up from his phone. "It is. It's pretty damn good."

"You're coming too, Parkinson," I told my so-called best friend. "If you threw me to the lions, the least you can do is be there."

Will's eyes went wide. "No, I told your mom I wouldn't be there," he said, still holding his phone. "I have a date, remember? With a guy you picked out."

"Well, not technically you don't," I said. "Not yet."

"But you've made a list and it's only right that I keep my dating options open," he said with smile. "It was your idea, remember?"

"Dammit."

"Yeah, your mom was disappointed too," he answered.

"Because she likes you more than me," I told him. "I can't believe you're making me have dinner with my mother, and you're not coming."

Will looked up the street. "Oh look, saved by the bus."

We got on the bus. Carter sat with Isaac and Brady, and I sat next to Will and stuck my tongue out at him, which he duly ignored. I hated it when he ignored me.

Will's phone beeped, and he gave me an uncertain smile and half a shrug. "Well, Jayden can come tonight."

"Your date?"

"Well, yes. You said to ask him," he answered. Then he held up his phone. "So I asked him."

"Jeez, you didn't waste any time."

"I can text him back and say we'll go somewhere else instead."

"No, no," I said, giving his thigh a pat. It wasn't lost on me that he said if his date wasn't coming, then neither was he. "It's fine. Guess I have to meet this guy sooner or later."

"You'll be nice to him, won't you?" Will asked, giving me a stern look.

"Of course, I will," I declared. "Scouts' honor."

Carter laughed in the seat behind us. "Mark was never a scout." Then he leaned forward between me and Will and quoted me in a whisper, "But he's fucked plenty of guys who were."

I looked at Will. "Not when they were Boy Scouts."

Will shook his head and stared out the window instead. "Nothing surprises me when it comes to you."

I sighed. "Isaac, I'm going to need to advertise in the personals. I need a new Alfred and Boy Wonder. These two suck."

"Well," Isaac said. "I can't vouch for Will here, but Carter certainly does. And very well, I might add."

I laughed, and even Will chuckled. "I can't believe I'm bringing a date to meet you lot."

I put my arm around Will's shoulder and gave him a squeeze. "He's going to love you, Will," I said. "You're all kinds of awesome."

"You think so?"

"Of course!" I said. "You are the company you keep," I told him. "And you keep company with me, and I *know* I'm awesome, so that makes you awesome."

Will shook his head again, but leaned into me and put his head on my shoulder for the rest of the trip to Oak Hill.

CHAPTER FOUR

SPENDING three hours at a blind school's art exhibition is something I could safely say I'd never imagined doing before I knew Isaac.

It was actually kind of fun.

Isaac was more caught up in the technical aspects of it all, for him and his students back in Boston, and he spoke to the artists and teachers there, sharing stories and talking candidly about what they did. Carter spent most of the time with Isaac, sharing in Isaac's excitement, whereas Will and I spent most of the time wandering around together and looking at exhibits.

"These are pretty cool," I said to Will, and the artist heard me. She was a blind woman who had a table full of various bracelets and necklaces.

"Which do you like?" she asked.

"The bracelets," I told her. "The embossed leather ones with the silver clasp."

"Ah, yes," she said with a nod. "I have very unique embossing tools that gives them that distinct feel. Those are very nice."

"I'll take two," I told her.

"Oh," she said, sounding surprised, given they were rather pricey, but she quickly bagged the two I selected. "Both for you, or is one for someone special?"

"Someone special," I told her, and after I'd paid, I turned and gave one straight to Will.

"Me?" he asked, sounding even more surprised than the woman I'd just bought them from.

"Yes, you," I told him. "Who else?"

"I thought..." He shook his head. "I thought it was for Carter."

"Nah, he has Isaac," I said offhandedly. "You're stuck with me now."

"Oh, that's right," he said with half a smile. "I'm your Boy Wonder. Minus the tights."

"I'm still not sure if you'll be given back your cape privileges yet," I told him. "But if you were to wear the tights..."

Will wrapped the bracelet around his left wrist and clasped it. "You can keep the cape."

I gasped. "No deserving superhero would willingly give up his cape, Will." I tried to do my bracelet up, but couldn't get the clasp to fasten, and before I tossed it across the room, Will grabbed my hand and fixed the silver clasp for me.

"Jesus, Mark, surely Batman can do up his own bracelets."

"Batman. Bat. Man, Will," I reminded him. "I'm not Magneto."

"Oh dear God," Will mumbled, punctuated with an eye roll. "Any other comic book characters you'd like to blaspheme?"

"No... Oh my God, Will," I cried. "That's an excellent idea! For Halloween, I'll go as Wonder Woman!"

Will blinked slowly, but before he could tell me how

awesome that idea was, Carter and Isaac joined us. "Oh, for the love of all things Marvel," Will mumbled. "Please make him stop."

Carter laughed, and Isaac asked, "Mark, what are you doing now?"

"Being awesome," I answered. "Will here has no appreciation for men in Wonder Woman outfits."

Isaac's mouth fell open, and Carter burst out laughing again. "Do we even want to know?"

"Kings is having a huge Halloween party this year, and I've been undecided about what to go as, but now I know. I'll be Wonder Woman. Will can be Superman."

"Really?" Will asked. "I'm Superman now? I thought I was Boy Wonder."

"Well, you won't wear the tights," I said. "And—"

Will put his hand up, cutting me off. "But Superman wears tights."

Carter looked at Will's wrist, then touched it. "Is this new?"

"Oh, yeah," Will said, thankfully smiling at the bracelet and dropping the lecture I was about to get about Superman and Lycra. "Mark just bought it for me. Pretty cool, huh?"

"It is," Carter agreed.

I held up my wrist. "I got one too." Then I took Isaac's hand and placed his fingers on the new leather band around my wrist. "It's embossed with some kind of pattern, but I don't think it says anything in Braille."

"Mmm," Isaac mused thoughtfully. "Yes, it does. It says 'Mark needs to buy Isaac lunch'."

"That's odd," I said, "because I thought the lady I bought it from told me it said 'Isaac isn't funny', but I could be mistaken."

Isaac laughed. "No, I'm pretty sure it says that you're paying for lunch."

"Well, just so you know," I told him, "I'm rolling my eyes at you." Then I took his hand and led him farther up the exhibition. "Come on, then. If I'm buying us all lunch, then the three of you have to do this with me."

Isaac stopped walking. He looked a little alarmed. "What is *this* exactly?"

I slid my arm around his waist and whispered in his ear. "I wouldn't do anything you weren't comfortable in doing."

Isaac shifted his weight. "Are you standing so close to smell me again, or because Carter can see and you're looking at him and smiling just to make him jealous?"

I chuckled. "Could be both. But he'll come over here now and put his hands on you. He does it every time, like he owns you or something."

Isaac sighed, or it was more of a quiet groan? "Well, he does, you know."

"They're walking over to us now," I whispered. "Carter will pull you away from me and put his arm around you. You can thank me later."

And sure enough, that's exactly what he did. He physically removed my hand, which wasn't even on Isaac's ass, and pulled him into his side, making Isaac laugh.

"What's so funny?" Carter asked.

"You're so predictable," I told him with a shake of my head.

Carter made a face at me. "Get your own boyfriend to fondle."

I glared at him and slid my arm around Will. "I don't need a boyfriend. I have Will. He puts up with me and doesn't leave me to move to Boston." I stuck my tongue out at Carter for good measure, then I pulled Will toward the door, where I wanted us to go. "Come on, you can be my partner."

"Yeah, thanks," he mumbled. "Glad to know I'm useful for something."

I gave him a squeeze. "You're incredible, Will. If anyone tells you any different I will need to kick some serious ass."

"You're so full of shit," Will said, but he gave me a smile.

"What are we doing in here?" Carter asked from behind us.

"Art class," I told him. "Painting, I think the schedule said."

"You can't be serious?" Isaac asked. Then he turned to Carter. "He's serious, isn't he?"

"Oh, please," I answered. "You do art with your students all the time. Carter brags about you nonstop."

"Yes, but no one in my class can really *see* how bad it is," he said quietly.

I laughed. "Come on, this will be fun."

We took our seats in what looked like an art class room, and while Brady slept at Isaac's feet, the teacher made her introductory spiel. For a small fee, we could paint or draw whatever we wanted, with one stipulation. We needed to do it blindfolded.

"I've done many things blindfolded," I said quietly. "But not paint."

Will nudged me with his elbow, silently telling me to shut up. Then Carter leaned over and whispered, "I have, too."

Will rolled his eyes. "No wonder you two get on so well."

We were given some large art paper and could choose what medium we wanted to use. I chose paint, Will chose charcoal, and we were handed paper blindfolds so we could experience a little of what the student artists did.

With my blindfold on, I was handed a brush, and two small cups that apparently had a different color in each. I didn't cheat and look, I thought the idea of doing this without eyesight was intriguing.

I felt around the edge of the easel and dabbed the brush into one of the pots of paint and started to make swirls, alternating the colors, broadening the patterns as I changed colors. I had no clue what it looked like, and it was fun. In a nonsexual kind of way.

When I'd done as many swirls as my attention span would allow, I pulled off the blindfold to look at my painting.

The colors were red and yellow and, subsequently, a lot of orange. The swirls were uneven and unsteady, but it was kind of cool. I'd always sucked at art at school, but thought my crazy high school art teacher, Mrs Bell, would be pleased. She'd think there was symbolic meaning to the flow or some other crap. I just thought I did well to get it on the paper.

It was then I heard Isaac chuckle, and when I looked over at them, Carter had pulled his stool to sit in front of Isaac's. Isaac had his hands on Carter's as though he was guiding him, like they were in that *Ghost* movie making pottery.

Not a great deal of painting was going on, more whispered words and giggling.

I shook my head and it was then I looked at Will's easel.

He'd chosen charcoal, so his drawing was lines in different directions and different shadings of grays and blacks. It was kind of smudged and kind of depressing.

It was kind of incredible.

"Holy shit, Will," I whispered.

He took off his paper blindfold and looked at his drawing. He gave it a dissatisfied shrug, then looked at mine. He spoke softly, "Yours looks like..."

"Like a kindergarten kid did it?" I finished for him.

"Give yourself some credit," Will said with chuckle. "Maybe a second grader."

I gave a nod to his. "Yours is amazing."

"It's okay," he said. "The lines aren't exactly straight."

"Neither is the artist," I told him.

He smiled at that, then looked past me to Carter and Isaac, who were still in a world of their own painting blue and red splotches in between giggles.

"They're very in love," Will said in a whisper.

"They are," I answered, just as quietly. "They weren't always like that," I added. Will gave me an odd look, so I changed the subject. "How about we do one together?" I took my masterpiece off the easel and replaced it with a blank piece of paper and then handed Will the red cup of paint.

I painted a yellow line, then handed the brush over so Will could add a red one. "What is this supposed to be?" he asked, looking at the painting and titling his head.

"It just is what it is, Will," I said. "It doesn't need to be *anything*, does it?"

Will shrugged, and his brow pinched, as though he didn't like that answer. So I said, "It's an abstract of Boy Wonder and his yellow cape."

Almost reluctantly, Will rolled his eyes. "We're missing his green underpants." He handed me back the paintbrush.

"And Batman," I added. "We're missing the most important part."

"Who says there needs to be a Batman?" Will asked, still looking at the painting.

"You can't have Batman without Robin," I told him seriously.

"No, I guess you can't," Will said quietly, and I wondered whether we were talking about comic book characters anymore. He was just so out of sorts lately. He was quiet and a little withdrawn. As much as I didn't want to be pushed aside, I kind of hoped he'd find someone that could make him happy.

I gave the paintbrush to Will. "What time is what's-his-name meeting us tonight?"

"His name is Jayden, and I told him seven thirty at the restaurant," Will said with a sigh as he added some more paint.

I wanted him to get excited, to be happy. "Are you nervous?"

"Not really," he said. He handed me the paintbrush. "Kind of dreading it, actually."

"What? No," I said. "Will, once you get there and he arrives you'll be fine. I'm sure he'll think you're great, and if he doesn't," I added, "then he's not the one for you."

Will looked at me for a long second, then turned back to our joint masterpiece. "Maybe."

Before I could say anything else, the teacher at the front of the class called for everyone's attention. Carter peeled off his blindfold and laughed at the painting in front of them. He told Isaac it was beautiful, though I thought it looked worse than mine. The teacher told us we were done, that we could leave our paintings to dry if we wished, and that we could collect them before leaving.

We had lunch outside, letting Brady out for a pee and a

drink. All the while, I couldn't help but think of not just what Will had said, but how he'd said it.

He was withdrawing himself. He wasn't happy here in Hartford, he never really was. He'd come back because of his parents had kind of made him feel guilty for leaving. He'd spent a few years at college in New Haven and moved back when he'd graduated because his mother whined at him that it was too far for her to travel.

Which was utter bullshit.

She was just a bitch who never really got over the fact her son was gay and had tried to convince him it was just a phase. That woman hated me. She thought I was the devil reincarnated, and she told me as much. I told her she was sorely mistaken. I was the *son* of the devil reincarnated. My mother already took that title.

She never acknowledged me after that, which suited me just fine.

Will visited them every so often, usually sans me, but if he wanted to piss his mother off, he'd bring me along. And I loved going, just to help Will annoy his mother.

Will's father was a silent, downtrodden man. I think Will's mother had broken his spirit a long time ago, and he never really said much. Will said he'd hardly heard his father say more than a few sentences in his entire life.

I thought my mother was fucked up, but his parents were a different bag of crazy altogether. My mother was overbearing, cigarette-smoking, gin-guzzling, Botox-addicted, ball-of-fun crazy. Whereas Will's parents were the horrible, soul-sucking kind of crazy.

It really was no surprise that Will loved my mother. She'd hug him and fuss over him and they'd do all sorts of mother-son things. He'd take her to the movies or buy her things from flea markets. She'd call me just to speak to him and in the end, I gave her his cell number so I didn't have to be involved.

But Will had been quiet these last few weeks. I'd noticed it and he swore nothing was wrong, but I knew different. I knew this because I'd seen it before.

It was the same kind of the unhappiness that Carter went through before he moved to Boston.

He was restless, and he needed a new life.

I understood that, and I loved him, so I was happy for him to go in search for happiness.

But Will was different.

I didn't know why. Maybe because I didn't want to lose another best friend. Maybe I didn't want to be left behind. Again.

And the only way I could ensure he'd stay in Hartford was to help make him happy. Hence the reason why I wanted to find him a boyfriend.

That in itself was a concept which didn't exactly sit well with me, though I put that down to not wanting him to move on from me.

"Earth to Mark!" came Carter's voice. "You in there?"

I sat up straighter and shook my head. "Sorry, I was a million miles away."

"We'd better get going, yeah?"

"Yep," I said, standing up and stretching.

Will was already standing. "I'll just go grab those paintings and stuff," he said. "I'll meet you guys out front." And with that, he was gone.

Carter, Isaac, Brady, and I walked back through the Center to the front doors, then toward the bus stop. "You guys just want to go home and chill before we head out again tonight?" I asked them.

Isaac nodded. "Sounds good."

"You okay?" Carter asked me.

"Yeah, I'm great," I told him, though he knew it wasn't the exact truth. He didn't press the issue, because Will walked up behind us with his hands full of rolled up papers.

"I can put those in my backpack, if you want," Carter said. Carter always took a backpack if they were going anywhere that Brady might need water or snacks.

"Sure," Will said, handing them over just before the bus arrived.

Will was still quiet when we were seated and had traveled a little while, so I nudged him with my elbow. "I was just saying we might go back to my apartment and relax for a bit before we go out again. Did you want to come?"

"Nah, I'll head home," he said.

"You sure?"

"Yes, Mark, I'm sure," he replied. "I need to go home and make myself all pretty for this date I'm having tonight."

"You make it sound like elective surgery."

Will snorted. "What am I having removed?"

Me, I thought errantly, *you're having me removed.* Surprised by my own thoughts, I did what I always did: said something funny so people wouldn't see the truth. "Your sense of humor, if you don't mind. Because it's faulty. Then you can have it replaced with the Mark Gattison Three Thousand. It's a state-of-the-art, high-powered sense of humor that has a one-hundred percent strike rate and can be used to charm others."

"Or offend them," Will added.

"Well, that depends on the circumstance," I told him. "It's a highly evolved program that can detect just what it's needed for."

Will shook his head, but managed a bit of a laugh. "You're a dork."

"Maybe, but I made you smile."

He nudged me with his shoulder and gave a sigh. "You're a good guy, Mark. I don't care what anyone else says about you."

I snorted. "Yeah, thanks."

When we arrived at the stop closest to my apartment, Will started off down the sidewalk in the opposite direction with a promise to see us at the restaurant.

"Oh, wait!" Carter called out to him, taking his backpack off. "Will, your drawing!"

"Give it to Mark," he called out. "He can keep it."

"Seven thirty," I called out after him. "Don't be late. You don't want Jayden to get there without you."

Even some twenty yards away, I could still see Will roll his eyes before he turned and walked away.

———

WILL WAS ALREADY at the restaurant when we got there. He was dressed in that gray-colored shirt that matched his eyes and his hair was styled. He looked good.

We sat at a round table, with me next to Will and an empty seat on his other side, then Carter and Isaac, with Brady, as always, at his feet. Will smiled and wiped his hands on his thighs. He was nervous.

"You okay?" I asked quietly.

He nodded quickly. "Yeah."

I patted his leg under the table. "You'll do just fine. Be yourself. He'll love you."

Will let out a nervous huff. "You guys all look good," he said, looking around the table.

"I'll have to take your word for that," Isaac said with a smile.

The waiter took our drink order and just as he returned with our beers, Will's phone buzzed. He read the screen and exhaled through puffed cheeks.

"What's up?" I asked. "Is he not coming?"

"No, no," he said quickly. "He's out the front. I'll go meet him." Will stood up, then looked at me. "Wish me luck."

I laughed. "You don't need luck. You've got me."

Will threw his napkin on the table. "That's what worries me," he mumbled before he disappeared out the doors we'd just walked in.

Carter was smiling at me. "Be nice to him," he said. "Try not to scare him off."

I narrowed my stare at him. "Oh, please. If some jerk can't put up with me, he doesn't deserve Will."

"So," Isaac said. "On an awkward scale of one to ten, how are we expecting this to go?"

"I'll be nice," I told them, a little annoyed that they'd think I wouldn't be. "I want him to be happy."

"Have you asked him what *he* wants?" Carter asked kindly.

"Well, yeah," I said. "That's how this whole 'finding Will a boyfriend' thing came about. I asked him if he wanted a boyfriend, and he said yes." Then I amended, "Well, he just kind of shrugged and nodded, but he certainly didn't object."

"Why can't he find his own boyfriend?" Isaac asked.

"Well, I guess he can find his own," I said. "I'm just helping him. He's not very happy here, and I don't want him to leave."

Before Carter or Isaac could say anything else, Will walked back into the restaurant with his date. Jayden was a bit shorter than Will and smiled nervously. Will sat himself between me and Jayden, and we tried to keep conversation going so no one was uncomfortable, though it kind of was.

I had to give Jayden credit; he was going on a date with a complete stranger and said stranger's three friends. Regardless that my cousin Chelsea reassured him we were normal, that still had to take some balls.

He was okay looking: he had short brown, curly hair and big brown eyes. He was twenty-five and was assistant manager of some clothing store, which explained his outfit. Not that it was bad, it just wasn't anything I'd wear. Granted, jeans were universal, but the plaid shirt was hokey, brand name or not.

It also explained how my cousin Chelsea knew him. She managed the shop next door, and the two had come to know each other, so Jayden said.

We ate our meals and talked about Isaac and Carter getting married and how their preparation plans were going, and then talked turned to safe topics like movies and sport. The four of us chatted, and even Jayden joined in every now and then.

I guess we got comfortable, and I didn't think anything of it, but when Will had had enough to eat, he simply swapped plates with mine. I picked at what was left on his plate, like we always did, as we talked.

It wasn't until the table was quiet that I looked up and saw Carter and Jayden were looking at me eat. I swallowed my mouthful. "What?"

Jayden looked between me and Will while Carter smiled and shook his head. "Nothing."

I looked at Will, and he smiled at Jayden. "Mark can eat more than me," he said quietly.

I pushed the plate away, as though it was the offending party, but the conversation never quite recovered after that, so before it could take a real nosedive, I suggested we make our way to The Stage.

When we walked out of the restaurant, Carter grabbed my arm and pulled me alongside him and Isaac, letting Will and Jayden walk some yards behind us. "Let them talk," Carter whispered.

I looked back a few times, seeing that Will and Jayden had struck up a quiet conversation between themselves, and they both looked happy enough. Jayden even laughed a few times, and I wondered what Will had said that was funny.

Carter was telling Isaac about his time in Hartford, where he used to live, where he used to go out, and the places he said he'd take him to tomorrow. "Isn't that right, Mark?" Carter asked.

"Huh?"

He snorted. "Were you even listening?"

"How can I pay attention to you when I'm trying to eavesdrop on the conversation behind us?" I asked him.

"Leave them alone," he said.

"I'm just concerned, that's all," I told him. "I'm allowed to be concerned. I seem to remember giving you a hundred questions when you met Isaac and you didn't mind."

"That was different," he shot back.

"Not really," I told him. "Because I'd have eavesdropped on you as well if I could have, but you were in Boston. So I had to *ask* questions."

Isaac laughed. "Did you give Carter the third degree when we first met?"

"Yes," I stated proudly. "It's my duty as best friend to annoy the fuck out of him until he gave me answers."

"Well, annoy the fuck out of Will tomorrow, but leave him alone tonight."

"Remember how I mentioned before about you getting married and losing your sense of humor?" I asked.

Carter snorted. "Yes."

"Yeah, well. That."

Isaac laughed, so I squeezed in between him and Carter and put my arm around Isaac. "Excuse me, Mr Brannigan. Pray tell, what is so funny?"

"You," he answered simply. "Mark, you know you're my second favorite person, right?"

"Well, you and I both know I'm your first favorite, but we just won't tell Carter."

Isaac shook his head and scoffed. "And you know I do adore you, yes?"

"Mmm." I considered where this was going. "You're about to insult me, aren't you?"

Isaac grinned. "Only because I love you."

"Oh jeez, it must be bad."

Even Carter laughed at that, and Isaac said, "You have full vision?"

Well, that was a weird question. "Yep, twenty-twenty."

"And you're of above normal intelligence?"

"I'd like to think so," I said slowly, still not sure where was going.

Then he sighed. "Just wondering," he said flippantly.

I looked at Carter. "Can you translate that for me?"

Carter laughed. "Maybe later," he said as we rounded the corner of a building. "Here's the theater."

———

THE CONCERT itself was pretty good, and when we left, Isaac said he was tired, so Carter suggested they go straight home. I looked at Will and Jayden. "You guys up for a few drinks or what?"

"No," Carter interrupted. Giving me a death stare. "How about you come home with us and leave these two to themselves?"

"Oh," I said. "Okay." Then I looked at Will. "Is that okay with you?"

"It's fine," he said with a smile.

Walking up to him, I cupped his face. "You call me if you need to," I said seriously, and then I kissed his cheek. I might have also given Jayden a look that said 'don't hurt him'. Then I tapped Will's face lightly. "I'll call you tomorrow. You kids have fun."

Just an hour later, Brady was curled up on the rug, Isaac was asleep in bed, and Carter and I were up talking, when my phone beeped. It was a message from Will.

Home, alone. Date was a total bust. I'll call you tomorrow.

I quickly thumbed a reply. *What did he say? I thought you were getting on okay. Did something happen?*

Said he wasn't interested.

You okay?

I'm fine. Call you tomorrow.

Okay. For what it's worth, no man who wears plaid is good enough to date you.

There was a long wait before he responded, *I love you.*

Without a second thought, without hesitation, I replied, *Love you, too.*

CHAPTER FIVE

I HELD UP MY PHONE. "Will's home," I told Carter. We were both sitting on opposite sofas with our feet almost touching on the coffee table.

"Alone?"

"Yeah, apparently plaid-boy wasn't interested," I said flatly. "Little fucker. How could he not be interested in Will?"

"He's a real nice guy," Carter said, peeling at the label of his beer.

"He is," I said. "He's great."

"What's his story?"

I sighed. "He came back to Hartford to please his mother who will never be pleased. He's been back here for over a year, but he's not really happy."

"So you're trying to find him a guy so he'll be happy?"

I nodded. "Yep."

Carter was quiet for a moment, as though he was trying to sort his words out in his head first.

"Just spit it out, Carter."

He grinned. "Well, what about you?"

"What about me?"

"With Will."

I took a pull of my beer. "He needs someone better than me," I told him honestly. "Someone who does the whole relationship thing and can make him happy. That's not me."

Carter nodded slowly, scratching his fingernail at the label on his beer bottle. "Still lovin' and leaving 'em?"

I grinned. "Absolutely."

"How's the scene at Kings?" he asked. "Still the same?"

"It's always the same," I said. "New faces every college term."

Carter shook his head, but he laughed. "You're terrible."

"I seem to remember you being with me for a lot of those nights."

"That was a long time ago," he said quietly. "God, I couldn't even imagine going through the whole pick-up scene again."

It was my turn to be quiet then. "You're really getting married?"

He looked at me, long and serious, then he nodded. "Yes, I am."

"How's Isaac been?" I asked. "He seems so much happier."

Carter smiled, and there was a softness in his eyes. "He is," he said, still smiling. "He's really working hard at it, you know. He's trying, and I'll admit some days aren't perfect, but Mark, it's different now."

I smiled. "I can see that."

Carter turned his beer around in his hands. "Since that whole mess with Joshua, he's more affectionate, more open. He talks about things that are bothering him. He includes me in everything, and we talk a lot more."

"Dear God, you sound like an ad on the infomercial channel."

Carter laughed. "I know, right? It's crazy."

"It's nauseating."

Carter laughed, then he shook his head. "I'm really getting married!"

I snorted. "Did you just get the memo?"

Carter still smiled, no matter how much I paid out on him. "I can't believe it, you know. I never thought this day would come, that I'd find *him*."

"Him?"

"Yeah, *him*. The one person I would want to spend forever with." He shook his head, like he could hear how utterly ridiculous he sounded but still couldn't stop the rainbows and butterflies shit. "I know Isaac's had his issues, and he still has them. Don't get me wrong, he's not some miraculously perfect man. Some days he's still the arrogant brat I fell in love with," Carter said. "But he's different now. I don't know... lighter, somehow. Happier. He still has his therapy, and he's really come so far."

"I can see that," I told him. "You both look so happy I could puke."

"Oh, nice," Carter deadpanned.

I smiled for him. "I get it. I do," I told him honestly. "Isaac's more at peace with himself."

"Oh," Carter said, tilting his head. "You *do* watch the infomercial channel."

"Only when I get home at two in the morning and I'm drunk, fumbling around with some random lucky one-nighter."

Carter shook his head. "One day, Mark, someone's gonna knock you off your feet."

"Hit me?"

He laughed. "No, idiot. I mean, you're going to fall so hard for someone you won't know what hit you."

I laughed at him, waking Brady up. "Not likely, Car. Never gonna happen."

"You'll see," Carter said, smiling as he finished his beer. "And when it does, you won't know which way's up."

————

ON MONDAY MORNING, I saw him walk around the corner and walked out to meet him. "Hey," I said. "Will, you okay?"

He looked around sidewalk. "Are you waiting for me?"

"Of course I am, asshole," I said, glaring at him. "I got here early to see you because you told me not come around last night."

"You had visitors," he said, still walking.

I raced to keep up. "Carter and Isaac left midafternoon," I told him. "You knew they were only staying until Sunday afternoon. I told you I could come around last night and cheer you up."

He shook his head and let out a bit of laugh as we walked into the lobby of our work. "Mark, I said I was fine. Really, it was nothing. So the guy said he wasn't interested. Who cares?"

"I do," I told him, as we stepped into the elevator. "I fucking do."

"Why?"

"Because, Will, I do care what happens to you," I said. "If some guy says he's not interested, then I want to know what's wrong with him."

Will laughed as the elevator doors opened and we headed toward our cubicles. "There wasn't anything wrong with him, Mark. We just didn't have that much in common."

I didn't exactly believe him, but figured he didn't want to talk about it. Which, with most people, meant I'd have to pick, pick, pick until they told me what it was just to shut me up.

But with Will, the key was to say absolutely no more about it and he'd eventually spill the beans because the silence drove him insane.

Which is what I did.

"I know what you're doing," he said from his side of the cubicle wall that divided us.

I smiled. "What's that?"

"You're waiting for your lack of questions to infuriate me until I tell you everything."

I laughed, earning a death stare from my manager. I gave him a wave and stood up so I could see over the cubicle. "I would never!"

He ducked his head and stifled a laugh. "You'll get us into trouble."

I sat back in my chair and snorted. "Believe me, getting fired from here wouldn't exactly be a travesty."

He sighed loudly. "Yeah, tell me about it."

It took a while—and some gastronomical incentives. I bribed him with coffee, gave him half my muffin at our morning break, and then even offered to buy lunch.

We sat at our usual table at the diner we often had lunch at, and after a little while, Will said, "Carter's a great guy. I can see why you two get along so well."

"He is one of the good ones." I took a bite of my sandwich and after I'd chewed and swallowed, said, "He's a lot like you."

"Really?" he asked thoughtfully. "If you mean we both put up with you, then yes, I can see that."

I smiled brightly at him. "That's exactly what I mean."

He ignored me. "Isaac's a nice guy too, though I didn't talk a great deal to him."

"He is. Isaac's a tough one. He's had a pretty rough life, which he's learning to deal with, but underneath the surface he's one of the nicest guys I've met."

"I couldn't imagine being blind," Will said, "yet he makes it look so easy."

"He does, yeah," I agreed. "He's a feisty one. He sure keeps Carter on his toes."

"I bet he does," Will said with a laugh. He ate as much of his lunch as he normally did and pushed his plate toward me. "What did you get up to yesterday with them? Take them anywhere exciting?"

"Not really," I said, picking at what was left on his plate. "Carter wanted to show Isaac around, you know, where he used to live, where he went to college, where he worked, where we used to hang out."

Will thought about that for a while. "Um, not to be rude, but how does he show him around, you know, being blind and all?"

I took a sip of my soda and shrugged. "He just describes it to him. Isaac's really good with sounds and smells and stuff, so he just lets him experience it that way, I guess." Then I said, "Carter's never treated Isaac any differently, really. Just treats him normal."

Will nodded slowly and smiled. "Well, come on. We better get back to work."

I looked at my watch and realized we were almost late. And Will still hadn't told me about what happened with plaid-boy, Jayden. I decided to let it go, figuring he really mustn't want me to know.

But it was about ten to five, and without looking over the cubicle or coming around to see me, Will asked, "What did you mean when you said Carter and Isaac weren't always so in love?"

I stood up and looked at him over the partition wall. "What do you mean?"

"On Saturday, you said they weren't always so in love," he repeated, though he didn't look at me.

I walked around to his side and parked my ass on his desk, like he normally did to mine. "Well, they've always been in love," I corrected. "But just not always that... happy or content. It's taken them a while to get to where they are now. A lot of hard work."

"They're very happy now, though," he said.

"They are, very much," I agreed.

"They broke up, didn't they?" he asked. "A while back? That's why you went to Boston that time?"

That was almost a year ago and I hadn't really known Will that well, so I never divulged much information. I nodded. "Yeah. Isaac had some issues with some guy he worked with feeding him bullshit and trying to get his money. Isaac was pretty horrible. I mean, he never cheated on Carter with that douchebag or anything like that, but Isaac can say some pretty mean things when he wants to. He doesn't really mean them, but he just lashes out. Anyway, Isaac might have had his reasons, but he was a jerk, and yet Carter stood by him."

"Why wouldn't he?" Will asked.

"Why wouldn't he what?"

"Stand by him. If you love someone that's what you do. Isn't it?"

"I'm not sure I would have," I admitted. "I just don't know if I'd ever compromise that much or go through that kind of heartache. Carter was devastated, yet he still fought for him."

"Is that a bad thing?"

I shrugged. "If it's real love, then it shouldn't be that hard, should it?"

"Are you saying you don't think what they have is real love?"

"No, I mean, yes, I do think it is," I said. "I just don't think it should take therapy and counseling for a couple to stay together." Then I realized how harsh that sounded. "I don't know... I mean, they're so happy and in love it's ridiculous, and truthfully, if going to therapy helps them, then that's what it takes for them and I'm all for that. I'm just saying I don't know if *I* would do that."

Will nodded slowly, thinking about what I'd said. "What exactly would you do for love?" he asked quietly.

I thought about that for a long moment, and when I looked at Will, he was looking at his computer screen and I realized he'd asked it as a rhetorical question.

He didn't want me to answer it, he wanted me to think about it. I frowned at that. After a long moment, I asked, "Will, what would you do for love?"

He looked at me then and it appeared he almost laughed, like it was a completely unbelievable question. "What *wouldn't* I do for it?"

He went back to his computer, typing out an email or something, and I went back to my desk. I stared at my screen for a while, not really seeing anything on it.

Something had gotten under Will's skin lately, and I was starting to think maybe I couldn't fix it. I hadn't noticed what was going on around me until Will leaned against my desk with his jacket on, and I realized I was late to leave.

"Shit," I mumbled, rushing to save the files open on my screen and shut my computer down.

Will was quiet, and when I glanced up at him, he was staring out the window. "I thought that Jayden guy and I got on okay," he said quietly. "I mean, we talked a bit and had some stuff in common."

I didn't say anything. I just listened.

"But when it was just us two, he asked me what was going on with me and you."

My voice was quiet. "He what?"

Will cleared his throat. "He thought there was something between us and said he wouldn't be someone's second choice."

I opened my mouth to say something, but was apparently too stunned to speak.

Will nodded and looked back out the window. "Anyway, I told him there wasn't, but it didn't matter." He stood up. "That's what happened. I gotta get going." He looked at my still-not-shut-down computer. "You all right?"

"Um, yeah, I'm fine," I told him. "You go ahead. I'll see you tomorrow."

He nodded and disappeared toward the elevators while I sat there trying to get my thoughts together. Well, that explained his reluctance to tell me.

And it also explained something else.

If Will was ever going to find happiness with someone, I needed to back off.

CHAPTER SIX

ON THURSDAY, I told Will he had no choice. None. Zero. Nada.

If he helped organize me having my mother over for dinner on the weekend, he was helping me go grocery shopping. No ifs, buts, or maybes.

Then, because Thursdays were a pretty good night to go out in Hartford, I dragged his sorry ass to Kings.

We'd had a few drinks, and when I pulled him out on to the dance floor and put my arms around him, it was the first time I'd seen him really smile all week.

"Well, hello there, smiling stranger," I said to his lips. "Haven't seen you for a while."

He rolled his eyes, but still smiled. We danced for a song or two, which was nothing unusual. We danced together quite often.

I noticed a guy I hadn't seen before watching us, and the more attention I paid to him the more I realized he wasn't watching *us*, he was watching Will.

Will, of course, was oblivious. So when he said he was going to the bar, I went over and introduced myself to the guy who was checking out Will. He was a good-looking guy, nice jeans, nice arms. He was looked fit and had short blond hair and a nice smile.

"Hey," I said, leaning in close. "I saw you watching my friend."

He was obviously not sure what I was asking for. "Yeah, he's cute. You're a lucky guy," he said.

I smiled at him. "What's your name?"

"Grant."

"Well, Grant," I said. "Tonight's your lucky night."

He looked confused, but when I grabbed his hand and led him out onto the dance floor, he came with me willingly. I turned around to face this Grant guy and put my hands on his hips. "My friend's name is Will, and he's a bit shy."

Grant pulled back to look at me, still confused. And just then, Will came through the crowded dance floor with two drinks. He saw me with my hands on some guy's waist and took a step back. "Oh, sorry."

"Will!" I said, reaching for him. I took one drink from him and pulled on his free hand until he was standing close to Grant. "Will, this is Grant. Grant, this is Will," I introduced them. Then I took the second drink and grinned at the look of shock on Will's face. "Have a dance, boys."

I sipped one drink and danced my way over to a table. I watched Will and Grant dance awkwardly at first, thinking Will would come over and abuse me for throwing him at some random stranger. But then they danced a little longer and I could see them talking, and I could tell from their body language that they relaxed a little more.

When Will threw his head back and laughed, I downed the second drink and hit the dance floor. I ended up in between two college girls, which wasn't all bad. They were kind of drunk and out for a good time, so I played up to them a bit, dancing in between them, letting them get their sexy on.

After I was all danced out, I took them to the bar to buy them both a drink when Will came up to me. "I'm going," he said. "I'll see you at work tomorrow."

At first I thought he was just going home. It wouldn't have been the first time we'd come to the bar together and he'd left early. But then I saw Grant over his shoulder, waiting for him.

Oh.

Will was going home with Grant.

"Oh."

He looked at the two girls beside me, whose names I still didn't know. "You look like you've got your hands full here anyway," Will said as he turned to leave.

I grabbed his arm and pulled him back to me. Our faces were close, and I looked right into his eyes, not really sure what to say. In the end I said, "You be safe and call me if you need me."

He nodded, walked over to Grant, and without even looking back, he left.

I turned to the two giggling pretty girls. "What will it be, ladies?"

———

I ARRIVED AT WORK EARLY, waiting for Will. By five to nine, he still hadn't showed, so I sent him a quick message. *You okay?*

After an agonizing minute, he replied. *Running late. Be another ten.*

I went around to his side of the cubicle and turned his computer screen on and logged him in. I pulled out his chair a little and put an open job file on his desk to make it look like he was halfway through something.

When our manager, Hubbard, walked past, he stopped. "Where's William?"

I looked up over the cubicle wall, shrugging at Will's empty seat. "Dunno, he was just there. Can't have gone too far."

Our manager gave an apathetic sniff, and off he walked.

Five minutes later, Will snuck into the office and all but fell into his chair. "It's okay," I said, leaning around the partition wall, whispering to him. "I covered for you."

Will exhaled. "Thanks, man."

"No problem," I said. "Care to explain why you were late? Did it have something to do with that guy last night? What was his name, Grant was it?"

Will cleared his throat and shuffled the papers on his desk. "Possibly."

I smiled at his embarrassment. "Possibly once? Or possibly twice?"

Will didn't answer, but he blushed, which was something he didn't do often.

"William Parkinson." I spoke low. "Didn't think you had it in you."

He shot me a piercing glare. "I didn't have anything *in* me. He did, though."

I burst out laughing and, of course, got busted. "Mr Gattison!" my manager snapped as he walked over toward me. "That's hardly professional behavior."

I nodded. "Sorry," I said, biting the inside of my lip to stop from smiling. "Won't happen again."

I waited until he walked off, then without looking over or around the partition wall, I spoke, knowing Will would know it was directed at him. "So, seeing him again?"

"Maybe. Said I'd call him," he answered. "Did you have fun with the matching Barbie dolls?"

Matching Barbie dolls? Oh, he meant the two girls I was with when he said goodbye. "Do you need to ask?" I asked rhetorically, not at all sure why I alluded to the fact I did anything with either of those girls. Because I didn't. I bought them a drink, then went home by myself not long after Will had left.

I don't know why I'd just said that.

I also don't know why I wanted to lie to him. I'd never lied to Will before.

I also don't know why the idea of Will fucking some random guy suddenly bothered me.

Then I remembered that I wanted him to be happy. This is exactly what I'd wanted to happen. So why did it sit in my stomach like lead?

"Anyway," I said, trying to sound enthusiastic. "You should call him. See where it goes."

"Hmm," he hummed. "Maybe I will."

And he did. When we were at lunch at the diner, he pulled out his phone across from me and called Grant.

Grant.

They made a date for Saturday night. Another date. That would be date number two. As in a *second* date.

They went to the movies, apparently. Had dinner and drinks, and from what I could tell, Grant stayed until Sunday afternoon.

Will didn't give me any details. Just said he had fun, they got on okay, had stuff in common. He didn't elaborate, and quite frankly, I didn't want to know.

Me, on the other hand, had the pleasure of having my mother over for dinner on Saturday night.

Let me just explain something about my mother.

Picture bottle-blonde hair, trademark dark red lipstick, a wine glass in one hand, a cigarette in the other. She'd married and divorced six times, was currently not-married, and although she'd never worked a day in her life, she lived quite comfortably off the rewards of her six marriages.

She held no regard for the sanctity of marriage; it was merely a means for profit.

Okay, so that might be a little harsh. But it was kind of true.

I know I've dubbed her Satan, which is also kind of true.

I loved my mother. I truly did. If anyone else called her Satan, I'd probably be pissed. As her son, I could call her Satan, but no one else could.

She was a fierce woman with not an ounce of maternal instinct, and I can safely say I spent my teenage years looking after her when she was between husbands, not the other way around. And when she was *happily* married, I basically looked after myself.

I guess that made me independent and self-sufficient.

It also made me realize I didn't need to chase love or have a significant other in my life to make me happy.

It certainly didn't work for my mother.

I knew it worked for other people, like Carter and Isaac, but it wasn't for me. I was fine on my own. Perfectly happy and well adjusted—though some would argue that—but I was comfortable with who I was.

So while Will was off having his lovey-dovey date with Grant, I was being tortured by my mother.

I'd spent the afternoon with not much else to do, so I cooked Mom's favorite dinner and stared at the television until she arrived.

I opened the door to the familiar waft of cigarette and perfume, and with a kiss on my cheek, my beloved mother walked in. She walked into the kitchen, pulled two bottles of wine from her bag, put one in the fridge and opened the other. Without a word, she took three glasses out of the cupboards, poured the wine, handed me one glass, and sipped her own. "Will? Want a wine?" she called out.

"He's not here."

It was only then that Mom looked around my apartment. "Where is he?"

"He's on a date."

My mother's mouth fell open and she looked like I'd just told her he'd died. "With who?"

"Some guy named Grant," I answered. "I kind of got them together at the club the other night, and they hit it off."

"What about you?"

"What about me?"

"Why aren't you there?"

"Will doesn't need a babysitter."

"No, he needs you."

"He'll be fine, Mom."

She shook her head. "Why aren't you on a date?"

I rolled my eyes. "Because I had to cook dinner for you!"

"Don't make it sound like I'm a chore, sweetie."

"You're hardly a chore," I lied.

"You're a terrible liar."

"Thanks. At least I tried."

Mom smiled. "You're such a sweetie."

I tapped my wine glass to hers and took a sip. "Learned everything I know from you."

Mom smiled and said, "Why can't you date Will?"

"Mom, we've been through this."

"Or someone like him. There has to be a boy out there that's cute and nice... and hung."

"No, seriously. Why can't you whine at me about finding a nice girl, getting married, having the picket fence and two-point-four kids like all the normal mothers."

"Because I'm not a normal mother, and you're not a normal son."

I had to agree. She had a point. "We are kind of awesome, aren't we?"

"We are," she said, tipping her wine glass toward me before draining it. "Anyway, you don't want a nice girl. You want a nice boy."

I put my wine glass down. "Mom, I like girls too, you know. We've been through this. Girls *and* boys."

Mom rolled her eyes at me and poured herself more wine. "Sweetie, you don't want to settle down with a girl. You don't want the mood swings, menstruation cycles, shopping, and her bitching to you about me."

"Don't I?"

She shook her head. "No, sweetie. You want a man. Someone to watch football with, someone you can share wardrobes with. Someone who loves me. Someone like Will."

"Mom..."

"Oh, please," she said, sipping her wine.

I took a mouthful of wine. "You know, I'm gonna marry a girl just to piss you off."

Mom laughed. "Then you'll deserve estrogen-fuelled psychotic rants about shoes and cellulite."

"Isn't that a little stereotypical?"

"Of course it is," Mom said nonchalantly. "Just like saying all gay men love cock and lesbians love to munch clams."

I spat my wine. "Mom, that's gross."

"See?" She smiled. "I told you, you don't want a girl."

I sighed, something I did a lot around my mother. "Why can't you be like other moms?"

She snorted. "Because that'd be boring, dear. Now, what's for dinner? I'm starving."

And that's how my evening went.

I heard all about the dramas in the country club's lifestyles of the rich and shameless, all about the short cruise she took with Gloria and how it's a terrible shame that the role of cabin boy has been made redundant over the years. She'd requested to see the captain, but the manager assured her there wasn't much he could do about acquiring a cabin boy that didn't involve solicitation. Mom was considering writing a letter, she said. "All cabins should have one," she said with a laugh. Then she got a faraway look in her eyes. "Though the barman was very accommodating."

"Mom, there is something called 'too much information'," I reminded her.

But she just laughed. "Don't be such a prude."

Dinner eaten and two bottles of wine later—me having two glasses, Mom drinking the rest—I called a cab for her. After she'd gone and I'd tidied up and sprayed air neutralizer, which was probably worse than the cigarette smoke, I checked my phone.

No messages from Will.

I typed out a quick message to him. *Everything okay? Call me if you need.*

An hour later, by the time I got into bed, I still hadn't got a reply. I was just about to send another message when my phone beeped.

At Grant's. Call you tomorrow.

I didn't sleep well.

———

I DIDN'T SEE Will until Monday, though he did call like he said he would. He sounded tired but happy enough on the phone, and when we were at work, I asked him for some details about his night at Grant's but he didn't tell me much.

The movie was good. Dinner was good.

"Is Grant good?" I asked with a smile. "Come on, Will. You've told me nothing."

"And I won't tell you anything," he replied cheerfully. "I'm not the kind to kiss and tell."

"You've told me before," I reasoned. "Why is this guy different?"

Will shrugged and turned back to his computer screen. "He's not, really…"

And that was all he said.

I had to keep reminding myself that this is what I wanted for him. This is what Will needs to be happy, for him to stay in Hartford.

So I would give him space. I would encourage him, if that's what he wanted. "Seeing him again?"

"I think so…"

"That's good," I said, sitting back down in my chair. "Let me know when he's ready to meet me."

Will laughed, as though that notion was a joke, and he never mentioned him again until Friday morning.

I'd asked him if he wanted to go out, somewhere different, I suggested. "It'll be fun," I added.

"Oh, well, I um…" He stopped, then started again. "I can't tonight. But what about tomorrow night?"

"Another date tonight?" I asked. "Jeez, Will. That's the third date. Things must be going okay."

He shrugged again. "Yeah, he's a nice guy."

"Okay, so Saturday," I said, getting back to us. "How about we do something?"

He looked at me and smiled. "Sure."

———

I WENT out on Friday night alone, not really sure what I was looking for or what I wanted. I looked for Will, realizing he never told me where he was going, and not finding him, I went home alone.

I didn't know why it bothered me, but something didn't sit well with me.

And after I met him at the open-air cinema in the park the next day, I realized what it was.

I missed my friend.

Wanting to do something I knew he'd enjoy, we watched *Casablanca* in the park. Not my first choice in movies, I'll admit. I prefer mine in, you know, color. With violence and sex.

But Will loved that kind of shit, so I suffered through it. I even sat on the grass with him and only complained about it once. Okay, maybe twice.

Will laughed at my dramatics. "For God's sake, Mark. We can go to the bar afterwards."

"Nah," I said, sounding not interested. "We can go back to my place and watch some Bruce Willis or Chuck Norris. Just to make sure my testosterone levels don't deplete entirely."

"God forbid."

"I know!" I agreed. "I'm rather fond of my dick."

"So I've heard."

"I'd hate for these romance movies to make it shrivel and die."

"You do know *Casablanca* is about the war, right?" he asked. "Hardly a romance movie."

"Is it a war with Bruce Willis or Chuck Norris?"

"Um, no."

"Then it doesn't count."

He laughed. "You're insufferable."

I pushed his arm. "You suffer me all the time."

He nodded. "Yes. Yes, I do."

"Well, for that, you can buy the pizza to take home."

"Let me guess," he deadpanned. "And the beer, too."

"Well, if you're offering."

"I wasn't."

"Sounded like it to me."

Someone behind us shushed us to be quiet, and Will laughed. He nudged his shoulder into mine. "Yeah, Mark. Be quiet. I'm trying to watch the movie."

He stretched his legs out in front of him and leaned back on his hands, getting comfy to watch the rest of the movie. I watched some of the movie, some of Will, and marveled at how one's ass cheeks can go numb from sitting on the ground for any length of time.

I leaned in to Will. "I should really have anal sex right now."

Will blinked and slowly turned to face me. "What?"

"My ass," I told him, "it's completely numb. I wouldn't feel a thing."

His whole body shook as he tried not to laugh out loud.

I shifted my weight from cheek to cheek. "It's not funny. I may never top again."

Will burst out laughing this time, and before we were shushed again, he jumped to his feet. He grabbed my hand and pulled me up and we weaved our way through the crowd sitting on the ground, heading toward my place.

One pizza, a six pack, and twenty minutes of *Die Hard*

later, I asked Will about Grant. "Have you met any of his friends?"

"No, not yet," he said quietly.

"Well, I think I should meet him," I declared. "I mean, I actually did meet him that night at the club, but I mean properly. Like we should all go out for dinner or drinks or something."

"Really?"

"Yes, really," I said. Then I took a deep breath and asked, "Do you like him?"

"He's a nice guy," he answered vaguely.

"That's not what I asked."

Will shrugged. "I don't know. I'm still trying to work that out."

"What's wrong with him?"

"Nothing," he answered. "We actually have a lot in common."

"Does he like chick-flicks too?"

Will threw the lid of his beer at me. "Shut up."

"What about next weekend?" I asked. "Maybe you could ask if he's ready to meet me."

"I could..." he hedged.

"Only if you want to," I said, offering him an out.

"I'll ask him and see what he says."

"Cool."

Will didn't seem so sure. And funnily enough, all week I was kind of looking forward to it, whereas Will seemed to be dreading it. But then on Saturday night, it didn't quite work out like that.

We decided dinner at a sports bar and grill was a safer option; there were flat screens showing different games of football and basketball, and there was music. It was more relaxed and should have been less awkward.

But it wasn't.

Will and I were there early, standing at the bar having our first drink, when Grant walked in. He walked right up to Will and put his arm around his waist, and standing too close, he gave him a kiss on the cheek.

And it kind of went downhill after that.

I was officially the third wheel.

An awkward, not-needed, out-of-place third wheel.

They included me in conversations, and Grant was a nice guy. He was polite and courteous, smart and even kind of cute, and he smiled all smitten-like at Will.

I didn't like him.

I also didn't want to ruin things for Will, so halfway through dinner, when Will said, "You're quiet tonight, Mark," I pushed my half-eaten dinner away and, feigning not feeling well, made my excuse to leave.

"Are you sure you're okay?" Will asked.

"Yeah," I said. "I'll be fine. Just not feeling the best." I stood up and pulled out my wallet. I threw a fifty-dollar bill on the table and looked at Grant. "It was nice to meet you," I said, giving him a weak smile. Then not really able to look Will in the eye, I just kind of mumbled to the table. "I'm sorry, Will. I'll call you."

"Mark," Will started.

I looked at him then. "You guys stay. I'll be fine. Honestly, it's just an upset stomach or something," I lied.

I made my way out of the restaurant and into the fresh air, if city air could be called that. And I started to walk.

I didn't know what was wrong with me. My chest felt tight and my head was swimming, but the farther I walked the better I felt and before I knew it, I found myself at Kings.

And, really, getting drunk was a fucking good idea.

I had my first two drinks at the bar, and when I ordered my third, some random guy came up beside me. He reminded me of the guy in the latest Pringles ad on TV.

"Where's your boyfriend?" he asked.

"I don't have one."

"Did you break up?" he asked.

"No," I answered, thinking that Pringles needed to work on his pick-up line.

"The guy you're always here with," he went on to say. "Or do you have an open relationship?"

"We're not together," I said, realizing he meant Will. "He's my best friend."

"Oh, right," he said, not looking terribly convinced. Not that I gave a fuck.

"Look, you want a drink, or a fuck?" I asked. "Cause that's all I'm here for, so if that's not your scene, then I'll save us both some time."

I didn't give him time to answer. I downed my bourbon and made my way over to the dance floor. Pringles would either follow or he wouldn't. It didn't matter to me if he did or didn't. If it wasn't with him, it would be with someone else.

Pringles didn't follow, but I saw him watch me as I danced by myself at first, then with some other random guy.

I needed to get drunk, and I need to get laid.

I needed to forget.

So I danced and I drank, and later, when Pringles made his way over to me, pressed his lips to my ear, and whispered, "How about that fuck?" I thought, *why the fuck not?*

We pushed our way through the crowd into the bathroom and into a stall. He kissed me, and I opened my mouth for him. It was everything I wanted: hard kissing, rough hands. I pushed him against the wall, fucking his mouth with my tongue. Grabbing my hands, he turned quickly so he faced the wall. He slid my hands down to the waistband of his jeans and popped the button on his fly. I slid his jeans over his naked hips and he thrust his ass against me. "Condom."

I rifled through my jeans pockets, but then stopped. I took a small step back and took a deep breath.

Pringles looked over his shoulder. "What are you waiting..." he started, but stopped when he saw my face.

"I'm sorry," I whispered. "I can't do this."

And I bolted.

Fuck.

I was drunk, but my head was spinning from something else entirely. I pushed my way through the crowd and almost fell out the doors onto the sidewalk.

And I started to walk.

I don't know how or why, but I just kept walking until I stopped in front of a familiar apartment block. I stumbled up the stairs and pressed the button for number eight.

I kept my finger on the buzzer until a rather pissed-off sounding voice answered. "What?"

"Will?"

"Mark?"

I nodded and finally breathed. "Yeah."

The door clicked open, and I went inside.

CHAPTER SEVEN

I TOOK the stairs and Will was waiting for me at his door. "Mark, are you okay?"

"I don't know," I answered. "I'm drunk."

He pulled me inside his apartment and led me to the kitchen. "I thought when you said you weren't feeling well, you were going home."

"I was," I said. "But then I was out the front of Kings and getting smashed seemed like a really good idea."

It was then I looked at Will. He was wearing sleep pants and had rumpled hair. "Shit. I hope I'm not interrupting," I said. "Is what's-his-name here? I didn't mean to interrupt anything." I pushed off from the counter. "I can go. I should go."

"No," Will said, grabbing my arm to stop me. "He's not here."

"Oh."

"I, um," he said, hesitating, "I told him I wasn't interested."

"You what?"

He shrugged. "It just wasn't going to work."

"Why not?" I asked. "I thought you got on well. He was nice..."

Will bit his lip. "There just wasn't any spark, you know?"

"Spark?" I asked.

"You know, no excitement." Will's eyebrows knitted. "It wasn't easy. It just felt like hard work, I don't know... I just didn't feel it."

"Oh man, it wasn't anything to do with me bailing out of dinner, was it?" I asked. "I thought you two were getting along and didn't want me hanging around."

"Is that why you left?"

"Not really," I said, still feeling a bit drunk. "I mean, I didn't feel too well, but I'm not sure it was anything I ate. I don't know what it was... I just felt..." I scrubbed my hands over my face. "I don't know how I felt." Then I blurted out, "I tried to fuck some guy at the club, but I couldn't."

Will frowned. "Why not?"

"I don't know. I don't know what the fuck is going on with me today," I told him. "I'm drunk."

"I can tell."

"I'm sorry."

"What for?"

I shrugged. "For just showing up here. For ruining your date tonight."

"You didn't ruin it," he said.

I shrugged again, not really believing that. "Can I crash here?"

Will nodded and smiled. "Sure." He walked to the fridge and taking out a bottled water, he handed it to me. "Drink that."

"You always look after me," I murmured.

He put his hand to my face. "Of course I do."

I grabbed his face and pulled his forehead to mine. "Don't give up on finding someone," I told him. "You deserve someone who's better than that Grant guy."

He looked at me, long and hard, like he was going to say something important, but instead he pulled away from me. "I'll just grab you blanket," he said quietly.

I dropped my hands from where I was touching him and he walked down the hall, I made my way to his living room and all but fell onto the sofa.

When I woke up, my shoes were off and I had a blanket over me. The shades were drawn to keep out the sunlight, and the smell of toast and coffee was coming from the kitchen.

Even hung over, I smiled.

———

"YOU'RE KIDDING, RIGHT?" I asked.

"Nope," Will said with a smile. "I'm swearing off men."

"Because of a few lousy dates?"

He sipped his coffee to hide his smile. "And I'm not going out just to watch you pick up random strangers."

"Then pick up random strangers with me," I suggested.

"No thanks."

He pushed his plate over to me and I picked at what was left of his lunch. "So you won't come to the club with me tonight?"

"No."

"But it's Friday!"

"Don't care. Still not going."

I sighed. "Well, then I won't go either."

"You what?"

I shrugged and sipped my soda. "I told you what

happened last time. I don't fancy having another freak-out in a bathroom cubicle. And I don't fancy seeing that Pringles-ad guy in a hurry. He must think I have erectile dysfunction problems."

Will smiled at the waitress who was standing at our table. "I'd like to apologize for my friend here."

She was an older woman, maybe fifty, with a hard face and badly dyed black hair. She spoke with a Russian accent. "It's okay. You don't need to apologize for erectile problems. I can give you the name of a doctor. He help my husband." The woman clenched her fist. "No problems now."

Oh dear Lord.

"I don't have erectile problems," I said quietly. "Thank you for the offer. I'm glad your husband can... that his..." I clenched my fist, but then looked at it as though my own hand had betrayed me. Will burst out laughing, and I shook my head. "That's not what I meant. Oh God." I looked at the waitress. "I'm glad your husband's okay now," I said, then I glared at Will. "I think we need to go back to work."

I paid the bill while Will cheerfully discussed dysfunction issues with our ever-so-descriptive waitress.

Hearing how rock-hard her husband was now and how his gonads would draw up before he shot his load damn near made me hurl.

Will thought it was fucking hilarious.

He laughed all the way back to work, and he chuckled to himself for the rest of the afternoon.

"I don't have *that* problem," I repeated, refusing to say the words erectile dysfunction to him again. "It was just one time, and it wasn't even *that* particular problem. It was in my head."

"Okay. If you say so," he mumbled, but then he laughed.

"I just freaked out or something."

Will appeared at the top of the cubicle. "You know I'm only joking, right?"

"No, you're not joking," I said. "You're being mean and very un-best-friend-like."

Will laughed and sat back down on his side of the partition wall. Then the bastard started to hum the Pringles ad song.

I stood up and spoke to him over the cubicle wall. "That's not even funny."

"Oh my God," Will said, laughing. "It is so funny. I'm actually amazed at how funny it is."

"I'm never telling you anything again," I told him. "And, all cape privileges are officially revoked. You were never cool enough to wear the tights anyway."

Will grinned at me. "Is that your comeback? You're gonna demote me to Alfred?" he asked. His eyes were shining. "Because the old guy had style. I could rock a three-piece suit and a feather duster."

"Well, you have the lack-of-humor thing down pat," I told him. "And I don't even want to know what you'd do to a feather duster."

"Oh please," Will scoffed. "I bet Alfred had it goin' on. He was probably secretly banging The Joker or Mr Freeze. Actually, Mr Freeze kind of had it going on."

"Well, I know what we can do for you, Alfred!" I declared. "How about I put one of your dildos in the freezer and we find out just how much you liked the big cold guy?"

Will's eyes went wide then darted over my shoulder, and even as he faced his computer screen, I could tell his face was going red. His gaze quickly darted past me again and he cleared his throat. The room had gone deathly quiet.

I turned around slowly, but I already knew my boss was behind me.

"Care to repeat that, Mr Gattison?" Hubbard said gruffly.

In that nanosecond, I tried to think of cable-related words that sounded like dildos or freezer that I could pass off as work related. I had nothing.

I cleared my throat. "Um, well, no, I'd rather not."

I heard a strange noise coming from Will's side of the cubicle, but didn't dare look at him.

"Something funny, Mr Parkinson?" Hubbard barked.

"No, sir," Will replied. His voice kind of squeaked, and he cleared his throat again. "Not at all."

Hubbard looked between the two of us. "I swear, I should separate you two."

And the words were out of my mouth before I could stop them. Or before I could think, apparently. "But we is like peas and carrots."

Maybe the Forrest Gump voice was the straw that broke the proverbial camel's back.

Because my manager clenched his jaw and spoke through gritted teeth. "Gattison. My office. Now."

Fuck.

———

"UNPROFESSIONAL, UNETHICAL, INAPPROPRIATE, AND JUVENILE," I said into the phone. Will laughed from the kitchen and Carter's loud laughter echoed down the phone.

"It's not that funny," I told Carter. "It's my second official warning."

"Your second?" he asked.

"Well the first was about a year ago," I told him. "It was

hardly an indictable offense. It was more of a social experiment."

Will laughed as he put my beer on the coffee table and sat down on the other sofa. "It was my first week," he called out, loud enough for Carter to hear. "I think he was trying to impress me!"

"Did you cross-dress again?" Carter asked.

"One of the girls on the tenth floor had been repri-manded for her wardrobe, so I wore skirt and heels to prove that George Michael was right: the clothes do not make the man."

"Or a woman, so it seems," Will said.

Carter laughed. "I take it your boss didn't appreciate your efforts?"

"Well, he didn't appreciate me taking off my bra in the lunch room," I told him. "They itch like a bastard."

Carter roared laughing, and Will shook his head at me. "Carter," he called out. "He only took his shirt off when I walked in."

I sighed impatiently. "It wasn't my exposed chest he liked," I said into the phone. "It was my ass in a skirt with tights and heels."

"Mark," Carter said with laugh. "What is it with you and dressing like a woman?"

"I am completely comfortable with my masculinity," I said proudly. "But here, talk to Will. I just remembered something."

I threw my cell phone to Will and slid my laptop around to face me. While he spoke to first Carter and then Issac, I was busy buying our Halloween outfits online.

Will covered the mouthpiece of the phone. "Did you want to talk to Isaac?"

"Sure," I answered with a grin. I took the phone. "Hello, gorgeous."

"I hear you got into trouble at work," he said. I could almost hear him smile.

"Yeah. My boss has no sense of humor. Apparently frozen dildos are not appropriate topics for conversation in the workplace."

Isaac laughed. "I can't imagine why."

"I hate my job," I told him. "It's sucking the life out of me."

"And not in a good way," Isaac added.

I snorted. "Nope. Definitely not." Then I said, "I just ordered mine and Will's Halloween costumes online."

"You what?" Will asked, almost choking on his beer.

"I just ordered your Halloween costume," I told him.

"I take it he didn't know," Isaac said into phone, obviously hearing Will.

"Not exactly," I answered. "But he'll love it."

Will grabbed the laptop and stared at the screen, and then looked at me somewhat bewildered. "Wonder Woman?"

"No, *I'm* going as Wonder Woman," I said. "Jeez, Will, give me some credit. As if you have the legs for boots and stockings."

Will glared at me, thankfully not able to hear Isaac's muffled laughter through the phone.

"Then pray tell," Will said seriously, "who the fuck am I going as?"

"Superman," I told him disbelievingly. How could he not remember? "I told you that before."

"But he wears boots and tights too!" he cried. "How is that different from Wonder Woman?"

"Wonder Woman wears a corset!"

"Superman wears spandex!"

"Lycra," I corrected him. "And underpants on the outside."

Isaac was still laughing, but I could hear him relaying the conversation to Carter, who was next to speak into the phone. "Sounds like you two are having the usual superhero conversation," he said. "Just remember, our wedding is two weeks after Halloween."

"Plenty of time," I reassured him. "If I end up hogtied on a train in the middle of the Canadian wilds, I have two weeks to get home."

"And two weeks for his hair to grow back!" Will called out.

I gasped, and my free hand automatically went to my hair. "You do that, Will, you shave my head and *you'll* be on the freight train to Canada, hogtied to a moose."

Will rolled his eyes and put his hand out, silently asking for the phone. I handed it to him with a childlike pout. He snatched it from me, shaking his head. "Yeah, Carter, it's me. Has he always been so juvenile?"

The doorbell intercom buzzed. I stood up and stuck my tongue out at Will for good measure. I pressed the button. "Ribs delivery."

Halle-freakin-lujah.

I got the cash, paid the delivery guy, and slid our dinner onto the coffee table. I held out my hand, indicating I wanted my phone back. Will said goodbye to Carter and handed me my phone.

"Hey, Car," I said. "You can stop planning your inter-vention on me for my obsession with juvenile discussion and cross-dressing. You and Will can save your fan-club banter for another day. We have ribs and football."

Carter laughed. "You're not juvenile." Then he added,

"When you're at work, you're very mature. But when you're not at work..."

"That's not fair," I said adamantly. "I can be just as equally immature at work, as today clearly showed. It even says so in my written warning. Juvenile," I repeated.

"You probably shouldn't be proud of that," Carter said.

"Yeah, well," I said with a sigh. "Hubbard can kiss my ass."

"I thought you liked your job," Carter said.

"Not lately." I didn't bother telling him I'd been a little out of sorts recently. "It's lost its luster."

"If you hate your job, then find something that makes you happy," he said.

"Yeah, like what the hell would I do?" I asked. "I'm a boring-as-hell structured cabling engineer, so unless someone needs a human sleeping pill, I'm stuck doing what I do."

Carter sighed. "Wanna know what I think?"

"That I should hang up and eat these ribs before Will eats them all?"

Carter snorted out a laugh. "Well, yes, that too. But Mark, you should quit and move to Boston."

"Carter," I said seriously. "The world doesn't need another unemployed comedian. You should stick to being vet."

"I'm being serious!" he said.

I looked at Will, who was oblivious to Carter's suggestion, and the thought of moving away from him made me feel a bit nauseous. Or maybe that was my stomach telling me to eat. "Carter, I adore you, but these ribs are hot and the Patriots are about to kick off."

"See? You even follow the Boston football team."

"Only because Connecticut doesn't have one," I shot

back at him. "Now be quiet. Give your man a big kiss for me."

I clicked off the call and threw my phone down on the sofa beside me. After I'd eaten a few ribs and the game had well and truly started, Will asked, "Are you really not happy at work?"

I tossed a rib bone back into the tray and licked the barbeque sauce off my fingers. "Dunno. Not really."

Will nodded slowly. "Are you thinking of leaving?"

"I don't know," I told him truthfully. "You're not happy there either."

"Aren't I?" he asked.

"You haven't been happy there for a while, have you?"

This time it was Will who shrugged. "I don't know."

"The difference between us is you still love engineering," I told him.

"You don't?"

I drained my beer. "I wish I did, then it wouldn't mean I wasted all those years at college for nothing."

Will snorted. "Carter told me they were years well spent."

I laughed and held up my empty bottle. "Want another beer?"

"Sure," he answered. Then when I was in the kitchen, Will asked, "What are you gonna do? With work, I mean. Will you leave?"

I handed him a beer and sat down across from him. "I have no clue. Carter thinks I should move to Boston."

Will nodded, and his brow furrowed. "Would you do that?"

I sighed deeply. "And leave you? What would you do without me?"

He gave me a sad smile. "Or your mom. What would she do without you?"

"Oh, man! Did you have to mention her?" I whined. "Now she'll freakin' call." And I swear, not even ten seconds later, my cell phone rang. I glared at Will. "I hate you."

Will smiled behind his beer bottle as I answered the phone. "Hi, Mom."

"Hello, darling."

"How are you, Mom?"

"Oh, I'm just fine," she said. It sounded like she sipped a drink. "Where's Will?"

"He's right here. We're watching the game."

"I thought you'd be out on the town," she said. "Why aren't you out having a good time?"

"I am having a good time," I said. "But we're not out clubbing because Will's sworn off men."

"He's what?"

"Sworn off men," I repeated, and Will slumped back into the sofa and groaned.

"What's wrong with him?" Mom asked, sounding concerned. "Did something happen? Is he hurt?"

"No, Mom, he's fine," I reassured her.

"Well, I have the best remedy for him," Mom said. "Next weekend is the Meadows Country Club annual open day. He can be my date."

"What exactly is an annual open day?"

"It's the annual fundraising day. Croquet, polocrosse, that kind of thing."

"Sounds like Will would love it. Considering he's never dating again, I'm sure he's free," I said with a grin.

Will glared at me. "What the hell am I doing?"

"Here, Mom, you can tell Will what he's doing next weekend. He sounds kind of excited."

Will's nostrils flared as he snatched the phone from my outstretched hand. He listened to the phone for a while, I presumed while my mother gave him a hundred questions. "Well, I haven't sworn off men permanently..." He listened for a while longer, then he grimaced and shuddered. "No, I haven't taken to licking clams."

I burst out laughing and Will tried to kick me. "Actually," he said, smiling into the phone, "Mark was just telling me that he was moving to Boston."

My mouth dropped open. "You didn't..."

Will grinned. "No, seriously, that's what he said... Yep, Boston... Well, no, he got another official reprimand at work today."

I threw a sofa cushion at his head, then launched myself at him. I tackled him into the back of the sofa and grabbed the phone. I might have used my knee and then dug my fingers into his ribs, but it was a win-at-all-costs situation.

"Mom?" I asked, pushing off Will and sliding toward the end of the sofa. "Don't believe him. Will's turned evil and is holding me hostage."

"Of course he is, dear," my mom said.

"Yes, and he made me eat ribs and now he's making me watch football," I told her. "I'm sure the Geneva Convention prohibits it."

"Yes, you sound like you're having a terrible time," she replied sarcastically. "Tell Will it's not torture unless he uses handcuffs and a spanking paddle... Now that I think of it, that's not really torture at all."

"Goodbye, Mom."

"See you next weekend, darling."

"Me?" I cried. "How did I get lumped into going to the old people's home?"

"It's not an old people's home. It's a country club," she scolded me. "Well, most of the people are old, but they have a bar. Like I said, croquet, polocrosse, that kind of thing. It's for the old-money types."

"The only thing *old money* about you, Mom, is that you happen to marry old men for their money."

I could hear Mom sip her drink. "I never said I came *from* old money, darling. I said I came *with* someone else's old money."

"You're terrible."

"Well, all of us country club ex-wives need a lot of money," she said. "Sex with the stable boys at the club isn't cheap you know."

I almost choked. "Mom! You made me spit my beer."

My dearest mother hummed into the phone. "Maybe you wouldn't be single, darling, if you learned to swallow properly."

"Goodbye, Mom."

CHAPTER EIGHT

I WAS STILL BLAMING WILL on the drive to the country club. It was a beautiful Sunday, and I was stuck spending it doing fuddy-duddy things. "It's your fault I'm spending the day at the old people's home."

"It's not an old people's home, Mark," Will said again. "It's a country club. They play golf and croquet."

I raised an eyebrow at him. "You're not helping your argument with that one."

"Mark, my dear friend, there will be polocrosse."

"So?"

"That means men on horses. Very fine athletes in very tight pants, on horseback... Do I need to paint you a picture?"

"I'm beginning to see where you're going with this..."

"Plus, your mom will need someone to drive her home."

"I think she likes you more than she likes me," I told him.

"Of course she does," he answered simply. "What's not to love?"

"You sound more like me every day."

"We're melding via symbiosis."

"You're such a nerd."

Will laughed and pulled his car into the lot of the Meadows Country Club. "Your Mom is meeting us here, yes?"

"Yep. If there's a bar, she'll be at it."

"Probably," Will agreed. "Discussing world politics and the ethical and financial reasons for substantiating fusion energy."

"If you mean scouting for a new husband while bobbing for olives in a barrel of vodka, then yes, that."

Will laughed. "Oh come on. She's not that bad."

"No, she's not," I agreed.

We walked toward the clubhouse. "You do love her, you know," he said. "I know you do."

"Of course I do," I told him. "She just doesn't qualify for the mother-of-the-year award. It's my job to be the ill-adjusted, bitter child."

We walked in, and there was my mother, dressed in her finest, waving a martini at us. "Yoo-hoo, boys!"

"Mom." I kissed her cheek. "Isn't twelve o'clock a bit early for martinis?"

"It has fruit in it," she said, holding up the glass.

"Not sure if olives count when they're pickled."

"Well, they should. They're green."

"Fair point," Will said, kissing her cheek. "Mark's been complaining all morning."

"For the love of God, go get him a drink," she told him. "Make it a stiff one. In actual fact, get him anything stiff—"

"Mom," I cut her off. "No sex talk before lunch. Remember the mother/son rules I stuck to the fridge when I was ten?"

She rolled her eyes. "Anyway," she said, changing the

subject, "we're out under the marquee. The polo boys are... warming up."

"I'll get the first drinks. Meet you out there," Will said and disappeared toward the bar.

"Will is such a sweet boy," she said, interlocking her arm with mine. "I wish you'd just get over yourself, get him drunk, and take advantage of him. You really should be together. You're the perfect couple."

"Thanks for the tips on how to catch your dream date," I said sarcastically. "But Mom, you know things aren't like that between Will and me."

She raised one eyebrow. Well, she tried. Botox made it hard. "Mm hm."

"Don't start on that again," I said, grateful Will wasn't here to be embarrassed again.

"He's such a doll. Can't you just be... what do they call it these days? Fuck buddies?"

"Mom, please don't go there."

"Oh please," she said. "I'm no prude, Mark. You know I've had plenty of booty calls in my time. That's what we used to call them back in my day, booty calls."

I stuck my fingers in my ears. "La la la, we are not having this conversation, la la la."

"Oh, Mark," she said, rolling her eyes. "You're the prude."

I snorted. I was the least prudish person I knew. Apart from my mother. She had that title categorically won. I mean, Jesus, when I'd admitted to her I liked both boys and girls, she was over the moon. The more the merrier, she'd said.

Mom and I wandered over to the marquee and watched the polocrosse guys warm up. I had to admit, it was interesting to watch. And by interesting, I meant hot.

The men wore white pants, tight like baseball, and dark green tops which were as tight as their pants. It was easy to tell why my mother watched this sport.

A guy stood beside me and my mother; he was at least in his sixties and wore an expensive suit and had expensive teeth and hair. "Such fine animals," he said. "Finest thoroughbreds, turn on a dime, amazing strength and they handle like a dream."

My mother didn't even look at the man. "They sure are."

Then he leaned in and whispered to her, "I'm talking about the horses."

Mom giggled, and the guy grinned back at her. Dear Mary, mother of sweet baby Jesus, I just witnessed my mother getting hit on.

As they introduced themselves and giggled some more, Will finally arrived and handed me a beer. We—me, my mother, and her new friend—were all still facing toward the open field. "What are we watching?" he asked.

"Just appreciating these impressive stallions," I told him. "And their horses."

Will smiled as he sipped his beer. "Well, the view is rather spectacular."

"How come we've never been here before?" I asked.

"So I could keep the handsome men for myself," my mother answered, still smiling at the George Hamilton lookalike, and of course, he never took his eyes off her and grinned a blinding, teeth-whitened smile.

Then George-wannabe-Hamilton looked at me and Will. "Do you mind if I take your sister over to see the horses?"

Will answered, while I vomited a little in my mouth. "Be our guest."

I faked a smile and pointed my beer bottle at him. "You have her home by nine, you hear, young man?" I said, which made them both laugh as they walked away.

When they'd gone out of earshot, Will snorted. "Well, that was weird."

"That was therapy inducing."

We moved closer to the fence, still watching as the polocrosse boys warmed up. They stretched and posed for the crowd, and when they finally mounted their horses, they had a captive audience.

I noticed Will staring, looking rather intently on one of the guys in particular.

"Like what you see?" I asked, giving a pointed nod to the man with the number three on his shirt.

He was a tanned man, maybe early thirties, with black hair and dark eyes. He wasn't the typical tall, dark, and handsome—he was stockier—but most significantly, he seemed to have caught the eye of Will.

"He's... there's something about him," Will said.

I looked back at the guy with number three plastered all over. He didn't seem like someone Will would go for.

"He's not really your type, is he?" I asked, going for nonchalant. "Anyway, I thought you had sworn off men."

"Maybe." Without taking his eyes off the polocrosse guy, he asked, "Don't you think he's cute?"

"No."

Will snorted, then he looked at me. "Really?"

"Yes, really. He's not my type at all."

I don't know why I was so against the guy, but my opinion only seemed to worsen the more Will stared at him. Soon the men were all on their horses and giving the audience something to look at by prancing near the fence in front of us.

And then it happened.

Number Three rode his horse over toward the crowd and stopped in front of us—and locked eyes with Will.

His horse shied away a bit, but he pulled back hard on the reins, controlling the huge animal easily.

And still, he never took his eyes of Will.

Will gave him a smile, and Number Three pulled on the reins again, leading his horse away.

"Well," I said flatly. "Seems you're not the only interested one."

Will finished his beer and handed me his empty bottle. He grinned at me. "Refill."

I looked back out over to where the polocrosse players were. "Yes, God forbid you miss anything."

Will waggled his eyebrows at me. "I think I might have a new favorite sport."

"Looks like it," I said, trying to smile. I held up his empty bottle. "Same again?"

"Yeah, I can only have one or two more if I'm driving home."

"I can drive if you want me to," I told him.

"You," he said, raising one eyebrow at me, "don't have a driver's license."

"I do so have a license. I just don't have a car."

Will rolled his eyes and turned back to watch Number Three prance around on his pony. Okay, well, it was bigger than a pony. Okay, it was huge. The horse was a mountain of an animal, and I wondered briefly if he compensated with the size of his horse because he lacked size somewhere else. Happier with that thought, I smiled and made my way to the bar.

When I came back with our drinks, Will was still

watching the men on horses. He watched them while they warmed up, and then he watched them play.

I'd never seen a game of polocrosse before. It was kind of like field hockey, only on horseback. And I had to admit, it was kind of cool.

I just didn't like it.

Okay, so that wasn't fair.

I didn't have anything against the other seven men or horses out there, I just had something against one of them. And his horse.

I didn't like the way he flexed his hips in the saddle or how he flexed his arms, and I really didn't like how he looked over at Will every once in a while.

During the final quarter of the match, I sent Will into the bar for fresh drinks, and when Number Three looked over, he scanned the crowd, obviously looking for Will. Instead he found me. I gave him a smile and a wave and an epic fucking eye roll, and my mother's voice sounded beside me. "Mark, stop antagonizing the man on the horse, dear."

"He's a douche."

Mom snorted out a laugh. "Yes, I can tell. The way he fills that uniform is just disgraceful."

I ignored her sarcastic remark.

So Mom added, "And the way he's been eyeing Will..."

"Like he's a piece of meat," I said. "It's shameful."

Mom almost chocked on an olive. "That's rich coming from you, darling. Sounds like someone might want him for himself?"

"Jealous?" I asked. "Not likely. Why the hell would I want with a guy who smells like horse sweat," I said, giving a nod to Number Three.

Mom smiled into her martini glass. "I wasn't talking about him, darling."

Good lord, how much had she had to drink? I shook my head. "Then who are you talking about?"

Just then, Will was suddenly beside me and handed me a beer.

"Oh, Will sweetie, we were just talking about you."

I sighed, and Will looked at me curiously. "Do I want to know?"

"No," I answered quickly. "Mom here was just talking about how alcohol affects brain functions and makes her say stupid things."

Will laughed, apparently very used to random, nonsensical conversations between me and my mother. "So where's the guy you've been talking to?" Will asked her.

"He's buying another round of drinks," she said. "I even suggested something non-alcoholic!"

I stared at her. "Jeez. He must be special."

"He could be," Mom said with a faraway smile. "He's very charming."

Great.

Here comes husband number six. Or was it seven? Before I could ask as much, Will nudged me with his elbow. George-wannabe-Hamilton walked up to us, and with a smile, handed Mom a tonic spritzer.

Will leaned into me. "Leave her alone," he whispered. "She's happy."

I looked at him and shook my head. "No, that's just the plastic surgery. She always looks like that."

Will chuckled. "You're terrible."

George-wannabe-Hamilton kissed my mother on the back of her hand, said goodbye to me and Will, and walked off. "Where's he going?" I asked.

"Just off to catch up with some colleagues," she said. We all watched as he walked up to three other guys his age and shook hands. Mom sighed dreamily. "He'll be back."

Then something happened in the polocrosse match because everyone around us applauded, so we turned back to watch the remainder of the game.

Number Three's team won, and when they'd dismounted and were talking with the other players and some spectators, Number Three spent most of the time looking at Will.

"Jesus, could he be any more obvious?" I muttered.

And because the universe hates me, Number Three looked at Will and excusing himself from whoever he was talking to, he started walking over.

"Apparently that's a yes," Will said, fighting a smile.

"Hey," Number Three said to Will, ignoring the rest of us. "Couldn't help but notice you looking."

I scoffed at that because *he* was the one looking, and Will kicked my foot. "Ignore my friend here," Will said. "He was dropped on his head many times as a child."

"Don't blame me," Mom interjected. "He was slippery."

Number Three smiled, and I wanted to die of embarrassment. Or junk punch him. I couldn't decide.

"Did you want to come over," Number Three asked Will, "and have a look at my horse?"

Fuck, what was Will? Five?

"Can I?" Will answered. Like he was five.

I sighed. Will gave me a quick look that was a little bit excitement and a lot of 'behave yourself'. "Won't be long," he said.

And with that, Mom and I watched Will walk across the field with Number Three.

Fuck.

"You shouldn't let him go, you know," Mom said quietly.

"What?"

"Will," she clarified. "He's your good thing, and you're just watching him walk away with another man."

"Mom..." I said with sigh. "We've been through this."

"Oh, I know what you've told me," she said. "But you and Will should be together."

"He needs someone else, Mom. Not me. I'm not cut out for that kind of thing."

"I don't believe that, darling."

"What's not to believe?" I asked. "You either want love or you don't. I fit rather comfortably into the latter, thank you very much."

"Don't give up on love," she said. "Don't be miserable your whole life like me, Mark. Don't live like me."

"Mom, you've been married six times. It was true love each time, remember?"

She scoffed. "I thought they were what I wanted, darling. I thought they could make me happy, but the truth was I just couldn't be by myself. You can. You're somehow a perfectly well-adjusted person, which is remarkable considering I'm your mother. You're quite happy now to be by yourself, but you won't always be."

"I am happy, Mom."

She exhaled loudly and looked over to where Will and Number Three were standing near the horses, talking. "How does that make you feel?"

"How does what make me feel?"

"Seeing him with someone else?"

I watched Will for a moment. He was touching the neck of the horse but looking at Number Three, and they were talking and smiling. It made me feel... "I don't know how it makes me feel," I answered honestly.

Mom nodded and gave me a sad smile. "That's what I thought."

"I just want him to be happy."

"I know you do, sweetheart. That's because you're a good man."

It wasn't often my mother and I were serious, but when we were, it was honest and open. We watched Will take out his phone and hand it to Number Three.

"What's he doing?" Mom asked.

"Putting his phone number in Will's phone," I answered quietly. I could feel Mom's eyes burning into the side of my head, but I didn't dare look at her.

The crowd was dispersing, and George-wannabe-Hamilton walked back over. A few seconds later, Will joined us as well, trying not to smile.

"Well," George said. "I believe I should introduce myself formally. I'm Ted Sinclair," he said, holding out his hand.

"Mark Gattison," I answered, shaking his hand.

"If it's all right with you, Mark, I'd like to drive your mother home."

I stared at him. I'd never been asked before. I couldn't even think of anything funny to say. "Sure."

I kissed Mom's cheek and then Will did the same, and we watched them walk away.

"So," I said casually. "You got Number Three's phone number?"

"Number Three?"

I looked over to where the polocrosse players had been. "Yeah you know, the guy you just spent the last two hours ogling with the number three on his shirt?"

Will blushed. "Oh, yeah, I did. And a date on Wednesday night."

I blinked back my surprise. "Jeez, that was fast."

"He does shift work," Will said. "He has Wednesday night free."

We started walking back to the parking lot. "What does he do?"

Will grinned. "He's a fireman."

I rolled my eyes. "Of course he is," I said flatly. "So does Mr Perfect have a name, or do I call him Number Three forever."

"His name is Clay," Will said. "Clay Damon."

I snorted out a laugh. "Well, that's a terrible name."

"What's wrong with it?" Will asked.

"What's right with it?" I shot back.

Will eyed me cautiously. "Mark Gattison, are you jealous?"

I scoffed loudly and rolled my eyes for effect. "Of that name? Are you kidding?"

CHAPTER NINE

WILL WAS ACTING normal most of Monday, apart from the more-than-normal smiles and the not-normal happy-to-be-at-work-on-a-Monday thing, and as much I wanted to bring up Mr Perfect-with-the-stupid-name, I didn't.

On Tuesday when he walked in to the office, he was all smiles.

"Someone's rather cheerful this morning," I prompted.

But nothing. He still wouldn't say anything. He just smiled.

And after five minutes of torturous silence, I couldn't help myself. I stood up and looked over the cubicle wall. "Let me guess, your smile has something to do with Mr Perfect?"

His smile widened slowly. "Maybe."

"You spoke to him?"

"I did."

"Did he call you, or did you call him?"

"Does it matter?"

"Yes."

Will was quiet for a long, smug moment. "He called me."

"Still going out tomorrow?"

"Yes, we are."

"Is he still perfect?"

Before Will could answer, Hubbard's voice boomed from across the room. "Mr Gattison! Do you plan on doing any work today?"

"Just discussing the advantages of six-strand construction spun around a steel core against galvanized round wires, helically spun together to form locked coil strands of stainless steel cables." I gave him a charming smile.

Hubbard glared at me for a long moment, then he huffed. I was bullshitting and he knew it. "Of course you were."

"I swear on my mother's next martini, sir," I said, sitting back down at my desk. When Hubbard had disappeared and after about two minutes of solid keyboard tapping, I asked Will, "So will he show you his fire truck?"

I knew he could hear me, but it took him a long moment to answer. "Hope so."

We didn't really get a chance to speak again after that. I didn't really know what to say. We were even a little quiet at lunch, which wasn't like us. We never ran out of things to talk about. Ever.

It was never supposed to be like this. It was never supposed to get weird.

Not with Will.

I wanted him to find someone who made him happy—I pushed him into it with that stupid fucking list.

I wasn't sure, now that he'd found that, why it bothered me so much.

So when we grabbed a sandwich and walked to Bushnell Park, we still hadn't spoken and I just couldn't stand it. I had to think of something to say that wasn't related to Mr Perfect-fireman-horse-rider Clay.

"Did you like that Ted guy?" I asked.

"Who?"

"The George Hamilton lookalike that was attached to my mother on Sunday?"

Will laughed at my description. "Yeah, he seemed okay. He was rather taken with your Mom. And her with him."

"Yeah, she's moving in, the wedding is in two weeks."

Will stopped walking and stared at me. "Are you serious?"

"No, not at all," I answered, "but should we take bets to see how long it takes."

"Did you take lessons in cynical?"

"I did, yes. I was so good at it, I now teach 'How to be a cynical jerk' at the local community college. I can get you discount rates if you want. Just tell them I sent you."

"And sarcasm?"

"Yep, I have my Masters in sarcasm. I can get you a two-for-one deal if you want."

Will laughed again. "You would seriously charge me to take one of your hypothetical classes?"

"Hypothetical is an extra charge," I told him, sitting down on a bench seat. "And anyway, I have to make a living somehow. I'd consider prostitution, but it's against my moral standing to enjoy my work."

Will chuckled. "God forbid you actually like what you do." He opened up his sandwich, peeled off the cucumber, and handed it to me.

"I don't know why you order food if you don't like it," I said, happily eating the cucumber. "I'm sure they'd make you a fresh one without the cucumber."

"But you'll eat it," he said, biting into his sandwich.

And we were finally back to our normal selves. We talked as we always did—about random crap. We had a ten-minute conversation on the benefit of Frosted Flakes versus bran. Because really, no one eats that bran shit without adding a pound of sugar.

Will didn't agree.

So then the argument careened into a debate about tooth decay and obesity in children. For another ten minutes we debated back and forth, but he just wouldn't concede that kids are fat these days because of their parents.

"You can't just blame the parents."

"Why not?"

"What about the companies that sell the overprocessed crap, and the FDA that approves the chemicals, sodium, and sugars?"

"Well," I countered, "they can manufacture and sell any product they like, but it's the parents who buy it. If it's not in the house, the kids can't eat it."

"Mark, you do know it's cheaper to buy fries than a salad, right?"

"Well, I don't agree with that," I said. "I mean, I agree with what you're saying—it *is* cheaper. I just don't think that's acceptable. But," I said, changing my tone, "I still think the parents have no right to complain that it's everyone else's fault, when they're the ones who purchase the product."

"How about the advertising agencies?" Will asked.

"You know what's cheaper and faster than fries, Will?" I answered his question with a question. "A freakin' apple. Kids should try that sometime."

Will looked at me curiously for a long moment, then he looked left and right, like he was looking for something.

"Is this conversation boring you?" I asked.

"No, I'm just looking for the cameras and cast and crew of *Punk'd*."

"Oh, ha ha," I said sarcastically. "Very funny."

"You know," Will said with a smile. "If you had kids, you'd let them do whatever they wanted. You'd be the biggest softy ever."

"If I had kids?" I asked incredulously. "What drugs did you take this morning?"

"Answer me this," he said seriously. "If you had kids, would you let them eat Frosted Flakes? Or bran?"

"Oh, man," I said with a groan. "I can see what you're doing, but you're wrong. My kids could eat Frosted Flakes because to make them eat bran should be considered as child abuse."

"Mm mm," he hummed. "I'm pretty sure it's not classed as child abuse to feed your kids bran without sugar."

"It should be."

Will grinned at me, then checked his watch. "Come on, or Hubbard will fire your ass."

"Not before I tell him to kiss it."

We made our way back to work, and we were all back to good. At work on Wednesday, things were good between us. I even told him I wanted every sordid detail of his date with Clay.

I kept myself busy that night so I wouldn't sit there wondering what they were doing all night, by phoning my mother.

"What's wrong?" she asked, sounding rather alarmed.

"Oh, nothing," I fibbed. "Just bored. Thought I'd call and see how things with Ted are going?"

There was a beat of silence. "He's here, actually. We're having dinner."

"Oh."

"Where's Will?"

I knew that question was coming, but still dreaded it. "He's on a date with that guy from Sunday."

"Oh." She sounded surprised.

"Yes, apparently he's a fireman, too."

"Oooh, I wonder if he'll take Will to see the fire truck."

I fell back onto the sofa. "It really is uncanny how similar we are," I said. "I had that exact thought."

Mom laughed into the phone, but then she was quiet. "You okay, my love?"

"Yeah, I'm fine," I answered, though it wasn't the exact truth.

"Did you want to come over here," she asked. "There's enough food for you. Have you eaten?"

"Nah, I ate already," which was another half-truth. I'd had a bowl of Frosted Flakes for dinner. "Plus you don't need me crashing your date. How is Ted, anyway?"

"He's very sweet," she said, and I could hear the smile in her voice.

"I better let you get back to your date," I told her. "I'll call you on the weekend."

It was a pretty sad state of affairs when my mother and my best friend were on dates and I was staring at the TV. I considered getting dressed and going out, but couldn't be assed, so I clicked off the television and went and stared at the ceiling in my bedroom instead.

———

I WAS DYING to ask Will about his date. Dying.

And of course, he was tight lipped and gave nothing away. But he smiled and that told me his night went well.

"Okay, you're smiling so that tells me the date with Clay was good," I hedged. "But you're wearing your own clothes which tells me you went home, so it might not have gone *that* well. Unless he's wearing your clothes?"

Will rolled his eyes. "It didn't go *that* well." Then he mumbled, "It almost did."

"But you stopped it?" I asked.

"He did."

"Gattison!" Hubbard's voice called out across the room.

I rolled my eyes and sat my ass in my seat, trying not to think about Will making out with Mr Perfect.

He stopped it. Clay stopped it. Which meant Will wanted it.

Will wanted more with Clay.

Oh.

It's funny how much work you can get done when you're trying not to think.

The rest of the week was much the same. Will smiled, and he seemed happy. He'd get random texts and smile at his phone, and every time his phone would beep, my stomach would drop.

On Friday at work, I asked if he wanted to go out that night, but he said he had plans with Clay. So I suggested the weekend, but he gave me a sad sort of smile. "Sorry, man."

"Let me guess. He's gonna show you his fire truck?"

Will's smile grew. "Hope so."

"So." I batted my eyelashes. "Is Mr Perfect, perfect?"

Will rolled his eyes and ignored my question. He turned his computer off. He looked over his tidy desk. "Are you done?"

"It's five o'clock on Friday," I told him. "I'm so done."

"What are you gonna do tonight?" he asked as we

walked toward the elevator. "You haven't been to Kings in a while."

I shrugged. "I was gonna go out with you!" I pressed the elevator button. "But you got a better offer."

"I did," he said with a smile. "But we can catch up during the week, yeah?"

"Sure," I said, but the realization I'd been relegated to second best kinda hit hard. "Doesn't matter."

We stepped into the elevator, and thankfully there were other people in there so the silence between me and Will wasn't so obvious. When we walked into the foyer, just before we walked out onto the sidewalk, he grabbed me by the arm.

"Hey, Mark, are you okay?"

"Yeah, I'm fine. Why wouldn't I be?"

"Are you sure?" he asked. "Because you said I should start dating... I don't want to not include you, but it's just that Clay swapped a shift this weekend so we could do something."

"Will, it's fine," I told him. I gave him a smile that he seemed to buy as genuine. "You should go out with him. I'm sure I'll find someone at Kings to keep me busy."

Will nodded and looked at the ground. "I'm sure you will." Then he took a step back. "I'll give you a call."

I barked out a laugh. "Oh, Will, surely you can give a better brush-off line than that. Have I taught you nothing?"

Will gave me a half smile and turned to walk away. "Have fun tonight."

"You too," I said, and with that, we both walked away.

––––––

I DIDN'T SEE WILL all weekend. I did go out on Friday

night, but went home alone. I never went into some back room or back alley. I just didn't feel like it.

Saturday lunch I spent with my mom and her new boyfriend, Ted, which was nice and kind of frightening at the same time. Nice to see Mom happy, but frightening to catch them making out when I came back from the bathroom.

I spent Saturday night on the phone to Carter and then Isaac, both who found my mom's make-out session—and my subsequent need for brain bleach—funny. They talked of wedding plans and catering and honeymoons.

"Honeymoon?" I asked. "Where are you going?"

"There is no way I'm telling you that," Carter said. "God only knows what you'd arrange delivered to... where we're staying."

"You're no fun," I told him. "Can I know how long you're going for?"

Carter hesitated, then answered, "We're going for four weeks."

"Four weeks?" I repeated. "Oh, man, that sounds good."

"Still not interested in moving to Boston?" he asked again.

"I don't know," I answered quietly.

"You sound more interested this time," he said. "What changed?"

I sighed. "I don't know, nothing I guess." Then I told him, "Will's seeing some perfect guy."

"Is he really?" he asked disbelievingly.

"Yeah, why do you sound so surprised?"

"I just thought... you know what, never mind," he said, sounding rather distracted. Then I could hear his muffled voice say something to Isaac, then he spoke back into the phone. "You know, if you want to take some vacation time after the wedding—"

"Carter, I'm not going on your honeymoon with you, no matter how much Isaac begs."

He laughed. "I can assure you, you're not coming on our honeymoon. What I was going to suggest was that we could use a house sitter for four weeks. Take some time, have a look around Boston."

I had to admit it sounded like a freakin' great idea. "I'll think about it," I told him. "And Carter, thank you."

"Mark," he said softly. "I know you feel like Will's forgotten about you, but he hasn't. He's just dating some guy and it's all new and exciting. That part doesn't last forever. You're his best friend, and that part does."

I smiled into the phone. He just seemed to know what to say. He always did. "Thanks."

I wanted to know how long he thought the new and exciting part lasted and when it would all be over, but I didn't dare ask.

Unfortunately, it didn't take long to find out.

CHAPTER TEN

"HEY," I said into the phone, by way of greeting.

"Oh, hey," Will replied. "Wassup?"

"Not much," I said, stretching my feet out onto the sofa. "I just remembered something and thought I better call you, because I was supposed to tell you at work today and forgot about it."

Then I heard voices in the background. "Oh, where are you?"

"Out for dinner."

"But it's Tuesday," I said, like that meant something.

"I'm aware of that," he said, and I couldn't tell if he was smiling or not.

I figured I'd interrupted. "Sorry, it can wait until tomorrow..."

"No, Mark, it's fine," Will said. "What did you remember?"

"I was just talking to Carter and Isaac and they reminded me about getting suits for the wedding. I was just meaning to ask you about it, that's all."

"When is it again?"

"In five weeks."

"Oh." He mumbled something to someone else, then spoke again to me. "We can talk about it tomorrow at work."

"Are you out with Clay?"

"Yes."

"You never told me you were going out."

"It was a last-minute thing."

"Oh, okay," I said, not sure why it bothered me. "Have fun. Don't stay up late. It's a school night."

He chuckled. "Sure."

I clicked off the call and threw my phone on the couch beside me. I was pissed off for no good reason, and because I was bored and had nothing better to do, I stripped off and got in the shower.

The water was hot and steaming and my hand snaked its way over my stomach and down to my aching cock. God, it'd had been so long since I'd had sex—months, in fact. Longer than I'd ever gone without some form of sexual act with some random stranger.

I leaned my left arm against the tiles and rested my forehead on my arm, feeling the hot streams of water run down my back while I pleasured myself.

Though it was hardly pleasure.

It was just a release. A release for the pent-up, angry frustration that plagued me. I'd been so out of fucking sorts these last few weeks, and now that Will was seeing that fucking Mr Perfect, I just couldn't seem to get my head straight.

And that's what did it.

I thought of Will. And when my hand pumped and squeezed my cock, it was images of him that swirled in my brain—of what he might look like with his head thrown back in pleasure, what sounds he might make, how he'd feel with my cock inside him, or him inside me.

I came hard, groaning through my orgasm. It was a hollow release; I felt relaxed, but not relieved. I felt... confused.

I'd just jacked off to mental images of Will.

I was going fucking crazy.

I crawled into bed, and instead of thinking about what just happened in the shower, I thought about the weekend instead.

I was going to go out. And I was going to get laid.

———

"COME ON, WILL," I said. "Call Clay," I tried saying his name like it didn't taste bad in my mouth, "and tell him to come along. It'll be fun. I'll even let you two pick the bar we go to, I just need a night out."

Will seemed unsure. "I don't know what he had plans for..."

"But, Will," I whined. "It's Fri-i-i-i-i-da-a-a-ay. I need to go out and it's your best-friend obligation to come with me. I even suggested to bring along your boyfriend and am forgoing the usual third-degree dinner and opting straight for the drinks."

Will rolled his eyes. "I'll call him and ask," he said as though he were placating a child.

I grinned and when he pushed his half-eaten lunch over to me so I could finish off his fries, I asked, "How're things going with him?"

"Him?"

"Yeah, Mr Perfect."

"He has a name."

"I know," I said, popping a fry in my mouth. "I just think it's an absurd name. Why would someone name their kid after a type of dirt?"

Apparently that didn't warrant an answer or even an eye roll.

"Things are going pretty well between us," he said.

"Could he be the one?" I asked, batting my eyelids and puckering my lips.

Apparently that didn't warrant an answer either.

"Oh my God," I cried. "It's happening! You're losing your sense of humor, just like Carter did! You fall in love and bam! Nothing's funny anymore."

Will threw his scrunched up napkin at me. "Shut up." He slid out of the booth and I followed him.

As we walked back to work, I remembered. "Oh, I made an appointment at the tailor next Thursday after work for the both of us. I told him our sizes and he said he'd have them waiting but would adjust them to suit." Then I added, "Because there's nothing off the rack about you and me, baby."

Will stopped on the sidewalk and stared at me. "Baby?"

"Oh shut up," I mumbled. "Come on, I can't be late. Hubbard loves you, but he hates my ass."

Will tried not to smile. "Let me guess, he's the only one to ever hate your ass?"

I grinned at him. "Well, there are only a select few who have had the privilege of my ass, and believe me, there were no complaints."

Will laughed, but his cheeks tinted with blush. "That's not what I meant."

"I know."

"You have no shame."

"None. It was omitted from my DNA, along with my scruples and bad hair days. I simply don't have them."

Will burst out laughing as we stepped into the elevator at work and touched my perfectly messy hair. "Yes, it's stuck like that."

"It's called product, Will. You should try it."

He rolled his eyes so hard it probably hurt, and as we walked out onto our floor and to our desks, we got busy with work and barely spoke for the rest of the day.

At five o'clock when we were finishing up, I looked around the cubicle wall. "You nearly done?" I asked.

He was reading something on his phone and looked up at me. "Yep. I'm done."

"Will, are you sexting at work?"

"Is that really all you think about?"

"Um..." I pretended to have to think about it. "Yes."

Will shook his head, stood up and pushed his chair back in. "It was Clay. He said we could all meet at The Green Room if you want."

"I want." It wasn't a bar I went to often, but it would do.

"You'll behave yourself, won't you?"

"Of course!" I said, putting my hand over my heart. "I hereby solemnly swear, whilst in the company of Will and Mr Perfect, not to strip naked in public, not to have sex in public, nor to partake in any activities that incur an indictable offense." Then as we left the elevator and walked into the lobby, trying not to sound pissed off, I added, "Jeez, Will. Does that cover everything?"

He frowned. "I just want to impress him, that's all."

We got to the sidewalk and I started walking in the direction of my apartment, leaving Will to go in his. "Yeah, I get it," I said, not really caring if he heard or not.

After three or four steps, Will called out, "Meet us there at nine!"

I looked over my shoulder to find Will still standing in front of the door to work. I gave him a nod as my answer and crossed the busy street.

It wasn't rational for me to be pissed off. But I couldn't help it. He was supposed to be my best friend, yet dropped me like a sack of shit when a better offer came along.

And it stung.

By the time nine o'clock came around, I was showered and dressed, looking pretty good in my black jeans, gray tee-shirt, and black vest. I'd had two beers for social lubrication purposes, because I figured if I had to watch Will fawn all over Mr Perfect, then I should probably be in a better mood than when I left him.

Then by the time I got to the bar, I felt guilty for being an asshole to Will and knew I owed him an apology. I spotted him through the crowd, standing at a high table, and made my way over to him.

"Hey," I said. It was a little loud in there already, so I had to lean in and speak up. "I'm sorry about before. I was a dick and I apologize. I promise I'll be nice."

Will smiled warmly at me. "It's okay."

"Where is he?"

Will gave a pointed nod toward the bar. "Getting drinks."

I followed his line of sight and sure enough, there was Mr Perfect, looking all fucking perfect, at the bar. Just at that moment, he turned and saw us and gave us a tight smile.

"Is he okay with me being here?" I asked Will.

"It was his idea, remember?"

"No, it was my idea," I corrected. "You asked and he agreed."

"Mark..."

I put my hands up. "I promise I'll be nice."

Will looked a little put out. "I think I could really like him," he said, leaning in and speaking into my ear. "I want you both to get along."

I pulled back from him so I could look into his eyes, and I nodded. Clay was suddenly beside us with three beers, and he slid them onto the table.

Will took a step away from me, closer to him. "Clay, this is Mark Gattison. Mark, this is Clay Damon."

I held my hand out, which he shook and gripped my hand a little too tight. Instead of rolling my eyes at him, I smiled. "Nice to meet you," I said.

He gave me a nod, and we talked over the noise about work and other awkward ice-breaking conversations that were awkward.

Did I mention awkward?

Yeah. Awk. Ward.

I bought the next round of beers, because if I was going to get through this night, it wouldn't be sober. When I got back to the table, Clay had his hand on Will's back or around his waist or stuffed into his back pocket. I couldn't really tell, but he was standing closer and they looked rather coupley, and for no good reason, it just annoyed me.

I looked around the crowded bar to the dance floor, but couldn't see anyone worth approaching. So I had another beer, and then another and by this time the dance floor was pretty full and I was past caring what someone looked like.

I was just about to tell Will that I was going to find some lucky dude to dance with, when Clay announced he had to piss.

When Mr Perfect left, I grinned at Will and, grabbing his hand, pulled him toward the dance floor. It was then I noticed he was still wearing the bracelet I bought him. I wasn't sure why that surprised me.

"What the hell do you think you're doing?" Will asked.

"Just one dance," I told him. "Then you can go back to him."

Will just kind of stood there, not sure what to do. "Mark..."

"Come on, Will. We always dance. It's what we do. We've always danced together," I said and pulled him against me. "And what's-his-name can just get used to it."

Will just kind of shook his head at me, and he didn't really relax like he normally did. I noticed Clay back at the table. He was watching us.

He didn't look very happy.

I mean, fuck. I wanted Will to be happy, but the guy who was lucky enough to score Will as a boyfriend had to put up with me. I didn't want to piss Clay off, but I had to let him know that I was a part of Will's life too.

So I turned Will around so he could see Clay, and resting my chin on his shoulder, I waved Clay over, urging him to join us.

He hesitated for a while, but it obviously got the better of him because he made his way through the crowd over to us. I gently pushed Will into Clay, showing him I meant no harm, but then he did the strangest thing.

He slid his hand over Will's ass and kissed him, open-mouthed and deep, but he kept his eyes open and stared straight at me.

It was a 'he's mine, keep your fucking hands off him' kind of stare.

It was disgusting.

If he wanted to intimidate me or threaten me or even scare me, he really didn't know me very well at all.

When he finally took his tongue out of Will's mouth, I threw my head back and laughed. "Hey," I told him. "Can I suggest The Shed?" The Shed was a club downtown that catered to certain kinks. "They have a water sports room there. Because if you want to stake claims and piss on his leg in *this* bar, you'll get kicked out."

Clay glared at me, and Will blushed a little and wiped his mouth with his thumb. Even though Clay still had his arm around Will's waist, I leaned right in close and said, "I'm going. You stay and have some fun. I'll talk to you tomorrow."

Will looked a little confused. "You sure?"

"Yep." I was damn fucking sure. I looked at Clay for long second, then back to Will. "If you need me, send up a bat-signal or call or something."

And with that, I left.

I was absolutely certain of one thing: Clay was a fucking douche.

————

I SPOKE to Will on Saturday, just briefly. I was heading to my mom's and just wanted to check in with him. I didn't ask if he had plans with Clay or even if he was there, because quite frankly, I just didn't want to know.

I didn't speak to Will again until he got to work on Monday.

He acted like nothing had happened. He smiled to himself when he didn't know I was looking and he'd smile at his phone whenever it would beep.

He never mentioned Clay, and neither did I.

But I couldn't deny he was happy.

All week he acted like nothing had changed, and on Thursday, I asked what he was doing on the weekend. "There's some Japanese Samurai film marathon on at Webster theater on Saturday," I suggested.

"Oh," he said softly, "Clay has a polocrosse game. I was going to watch."

"No worries," I said, covering quickly with some excuse that I only watched those shit subtitled movies because he liked them.

But he didn't offer for me to come with him to watch stupid Clay on his stupid horse. I would have said no anyway, but it would have been nice to have been asked.

I wondered whether it was Will's or Clay's stipulation that I not be invited.

I guessed it didn't matter.

"We've got our suit fittings this afternoon," I reminded him quietly. Then something occurred to me. Maybe he didn't want to go to Carter and Isaac's wedding as my date anymore. "Hey, if you don't want to come to the wedding, you don't have to," I told him.

"Oh, um..."

"Anyway, if you'd rather not, I can find someone else to go with me. It's no big deal."

"I forgot about the fitting," he mumbled. "I'll just text Clay..." He pulled out his phone, thumbing out some message. "I told him I'd head straight to his place after work, so I just told him I'll be late." Then he said, "I want to go to the wedding. I said I would."

"Well, actually, you didn't," I told him. "I kind of told you you were going, and you just never said no."

Will's phone beeped, and our conversation was forgotten as he texted back and forth with Clay.

I told Will I had to work through lunch to get some figures done for a client, which wasn't exactly the truth, and when five o'clock rolled around, I packed up and left before him.

I'd walked the two blocks to the tailor, when Will called out behind me. "Mark, wait!"

He was almost running to catch up. "Hey, are you okay?" he asked. "Are you pissed off at me? Because I said I'd go to the wedding." He looked worried as he ran his hand through his short blond hair.

I shook my head and laughed at how ridiculous this was. He was free to do whatever he wanted. "No, Will, it's fine."

His eyes narrowed at me. "You sure?"

"Of course I am," I said, relieved that he still cared. "Let's go in and show 'em how to fill a suit."

We'd done little more than introduce ourselves to the woman at the front desk of the tailor, when the door behind us opened. I didn't turn around at first, not really caring who else walked into the store, but when Will spoke to someone, I looked to see who it was.

Clay.

In his blue fireman pants and boots and a blue tee-shirt with Hartford Fire Department written on the front.

Great.

Just fucking great.

"When I texted Clay earlier," Will said, "I told him we'd be here and wouldn't be long, and that he should come down if he had time."

I guess he had time.

Where the fuck are all the pyromaniacs when I need them?

So what was supposed to be a fun thing for me and Will

to do turned into a very quiet, very rushed, very shitty evening.

I told the tailor on the quiet to put Will's tab on mine, and as soon as the measurements were taken, I made an excuse about not feeling good and left.

And the truth was, I *didn't* feel good.

The more I thought about it, the worse I felt. So I spent the night on the couch watching reruns of *Star Trek*.

I told Will on Friday I still wasn't feeling great and that was why I was heading straight home after work. Even though he was busy with Clay all weekend, he did text me to check on me. I replied saying I was okay and stupidly asked him what he was doing.

He never replied.

At work the next Monday, I pretended to be busy when Will got into the office and it was midmorning before we really got a chance to talk. And because he never texted me back and because I'm so mature, I waited for him to speak first.

"How was your weekend?" he asked.

"Okay," I lied.

"Feel better?"

"Yeah," I said. I never asked him about his weekend. I never asked about Clay.

I just didn't want to know.

Because I knew, deep down, I was losing my best friend.

———

THE REST of the week dragged. I got an incredible amount of work done—actually avoiding Will and not chatting over the cubicle wall meant I cleaned out my in-tray and then some.

Hubbard even smiled at me, and I didn't say anything smartass back.

I spent the nights on the sofa, watching shit on TV. I spoke to Carter and Isaac on Wednesday, which was the highlight of my week.

I was truly pathetic.

By the next Friday, I was over it. Things between me and Will were weird, and it was awful.

I needed to get out. I needed to get laid, and I needed to find someone I could hang out with. The kind that didn't dump me when they found a new toy to play with. I didn't want to replace Will... I just wanted... well, I didn't know what the fuck I wanted.

So on Friday night, I got dressed up and went to Kings. I was earlier than normal, and the place wasn't too busy yet and I found myself at the bar.

"Hey, Pete," I greeted the barman with a smile. He'd been the barman here for years, and as a place I frequented, I knew the names of most of the staff.

"Mark," he said, smiling back at me. "What can I get you?"

"Just a Sams, thanks," I answered, and I laid out a fiver on the bar.

Pete put my beer on the bar. "Where's Will?"

"He's with his new boyfriend," I said, unable to stop the eye roll.

"Who's the lucky fella?"

"Some guy named Clay. Plays polocrosse. Fire fighter. Mr Perfect, apparently."

The barman's eyes narrowed. His voice was quiet. "Clay Damon?"

"Yeah, do you know him?" I asked, then took a mouthful of beer.

"I know him by reputation only."

"What? I suppose he's hung like his horse too. Please tell me he has a pencil dick."

He shook his head. "No. He's not a nice guy. He's a real prick, apparently. Has a real bad temper from what I've heard."

Another patron called out to Pete, and as he walked away, he said, "Had an incident here a while back with him. Roughed up his boyfriend."

Oh, hell the fuck no.

I remembered the disgusting stare he gave me while he kissed Will the other weekend, how possessive he was. I left my beer on the bar and as soon as I was outside, I pulled out my phone. I called Will's number, but it went to voice mail. "Will, you need to call me. As soon as you get this message. Please."

CHAPTER ELEVEN

PACING up and down the fucking sidewalk, I tried calling again, but there was no answer. Maybe Pete the barman got it wrong. Maybe he was thinking of someone else. Maybe I was about to make accusations that simply weren't true. So I walked back to the two security men at the door, Eric and Theo, and asked them, "Hey, do you guys know a guy named Clay Damon?"

Both guys kind of shrugged. "Name don't ring a bell," Eric said.

"He's about my height, browny-kinda-colored hair, good looking. Rides horses, plays polocrosse," I said, trying to explain further. "Pete behind the bar said he's a real piece of work."

Theo shook his head. "Nah, man."

"He's a fireman," I told them.

There was a flash of recognition in Eric's eyes. "We kicked a guy outta here about a year ago, told him never to come back. He was a fireman. There was a group of firemen out for a birthday or something, one of them got thrown out. I remember that."

For someone to be barred from Kings, they must have done something pretty bad. "What did he do to get banned?"

"Belted his so-called boyfriend in the back room."

My stomach dropped. Without another word, I turned and started walking to Will's place, and then I started to run.

It was a cold fear that tightened my chest and a sense of dread, and I swore to myself if that son of a bitch laid one finger on Will, I'd rip his head from his shoulders.

Even though I'd run the four blocks to Will's apartment, my adrenaline and good intentions for homicide were for nothing. He wasn't home.

I tried his cell again, but still no answer.

And then I started to panic.

And I could have kicked myself for being such a dick during the week. Why the fuck did we skirt around each other? If I hadn't have been such an immature fucking idiot, I'd know where he was right now.

Not knowing what else to do, I went to all the places I'd known they went to together. Restaurants, clubs, bars— everywhere I could think of. But couldn't find him. I had no clue where Clay lived or any of his friends' names. I'd never thought to ask.

I'd been kind of ignorant about the whole thing.

And I sorely regretted it now.

By the time I got home, it was almost midnight, I was stone-cold sober and feeling sick to my stomach. I'd left five messages all told, and he'd not replied. I considered calling Will's parents but realizing the late hour, decided against it. Although, I'd decided, if I hadn't heard back from Will by tomorrow morning, I'd call them. I'd go see them if I had to.

After finally falling asleep, I was awoken by the sound

of my ringing phone. I fumbled for the nightstand and seeing Will's name on the screen, I sat up in bed, suddenly very awake. "Will?"

"Yeah, Mark, it's me. What's wrong? I just checked my phone, and you'd left a dozen messages. Did something happen?"

I checked the time. It was ten past seven. "Where are you? I've been worried sick."

"We're out of town," he said. "I told you Clay had a game this weekend, so we came up a day early. What is it, Mark? What was the emergency?"

"I needed to know you were okay," I told him, scrubbing my hand over my face. "Will, I need to tell you something."

"Tell me what?" he asked cautiously.

"I think you should leave Clay. Get in your car or catch a bus or a cab if you have to, just stay away from him."

There was nothing but silence for a long while. "What?"

"I heard some bad things about him, Will. That he's abusive, that he belted his boyfriend."

Again, silence.

"Will, you there?" I asked. "Is Clay there? Where is he right now?"

"He's in the shower," Will said softly. "Who told you that? Who said that about him?"

"Pete."

"The barman at Kings?"

"Yes!"

"Oh Jesus, Mark, really?" Will scoffed into the phone. "He also takes twenties from the sluts out back for blow jobs."

I ignored that. "One of the bouncers said so too."

"Oh, for fuck's sake, Mark. You hardly said a word to me all week, but you were asking about Clay at the club?"

"Yes!" I cried. "I was worried about you!"

"You realize you sound a little crazy right now?"

"Will, I'm being serious."

"So am I, Mark," he said flatly. "Look, I'll call you tomorrow night."

And then I was listening to a dial tone.

Fuck.

I fell back onto the bed with a frustrated groan and lay there staring at the ceiling. In the light of day, I could see that maybe I did overreact. Maybe Pete the barman and the two security guards weren't the best witnesses. I didn't even really have proof.

I *think* they were talking about Clay.

Pete caught the name, and said he had a reputation as an asshole who once hit his so-called boyfriend in the back room. Then Eric the security guy said it was a fireman who got thrown out.

Even if I was wrong, I couldn't bring myself to be sorry.

Because if I was right, if Clay was the type of guy to raise his hand in anger, then warning Will was the right thing to do.

Even if he hated me for it.

I decided I'd wait. Will sounded happy enough with Clay, and maybe there was some confusion on my behalf, but either way, I would wait to hear both sides of the story.

So I tried to forget about it.

I had one of the longest, shittiest weekends of my life.

I was angry and lonely, never a good combination. On Saturday, I considered going out and getting smashed and laid, but in the end, walked down to the cinema and watched some latest movie about superheroes.

Well, that wasn't true. I paid to watch it, but sat there and stared at the screen, thinking about my life.

And I thought about Carter's suggestion that I move to Boston.

It was something I wanted to talk over with Will, but then it occurred to me that he might not give a fuck.

I hated that feeling. I hated feeling dumped. I hated feeling second best.

Carter had found someone, now Will. Hell, even my mother had found someone new.

So maybe I needed a change. Maybe a move to a different city was what I needed. A new city, new clubs, new faces.

I thought of Carter's offer to house-sit for him and Isaac while they were away, and by the time I got home, I was convinced it was a good place to start.

I'd take some leave from work and spend the time in Boston, see if it was where I'd want to live. I'd always enjoyed my time there when I visited, so maybe I'd see what the employment and rental market was like while I was there.

Will didn't call me on Sunday. Instead, I got a short text. *Won't be home till late. See you at work tomorrow.*

I turned my phone in my hands over and over, thinking of things I should say, questions I should ask.

Instead, I turned my phone off, lay down on the sofa, and stared at the TV.

———

IF THE LAST few weeks had been awkward between me and Will, then Monday was the standout.

I got to work early and waited out front for him. I was

strangely nervous about seeing him, wondering how the conversation about my accusations would go.

My heart thumped out of time when I saw him, and the closer he got, the more nervous I became. When he looked up and saw me, he quickly looked at the ground. He stopped when he got to me, but still didn't say anything and still didn't look at me.

"Hey," I said softly.

He cleared his throat. "We'd better get inside. It's almost nine." And with that, he brushed past me and through the front doors to work.

So that was it.

I took a deep breath, swallowed the lump in my throat, and followed him in.

Just like the week before, the next few hours were so fucking quiet between us. There was no banter, no laughs.

"Going for employee of the month, Gattison?" Hubbard asked behind me.

I swiveled my chair around to look at him. I didn't even pretend to smile at his attempt at a joke. "About that, sir," I started. "I was wondering if I could put in for some vacation time?"

I figured asking him in front of Will would save everyone from more awkward conversations later.

"When?" Hubbard asked. "And for how long?"

"In three weeks. And I'd be gone for a month, sir."

Hubbard frowned, and his whole round little face puckered. "Hmm, I'll check the staff allocation and let you know."

"Thanks," I said quietly.

He stared at me for a long moment, as though he couldn't decide if he cared enough to ask. In the end, he asked anyway. "Everything okay, Gattison?"

"Yeah," I lied poorly. "Just fine." I turned my chair back to my desk, not caring if he believed me or not. I didn't watch him leave.

Instead, I stood up and headed to the men's room. I leaned against the sink and pulled my phone from my pocket. I sent Carter a text, telling him they had a house sitter.

The bathroom door opened, and Will stopped when he saw me. He closed the door and leaned against it. He looked confused. "Are you leaving for a month?"

"Yeah," I answered. "I need some..." Then I corrected myself. "Carter and Isaac need a house sitter and someone to mind the dog and cat while they're away."

He nodded slowly. "Mark, I—"

I put my hand up to stop him. "Will, it's fine. You don't have to come to the wedding if you don't want. Actually, the way things have been lately, it's probably best if you didn't come."

I walked over to him and, grabbing the door handle, had to wait for him to step aside so I could open the door.

I'm not sure why I said that. I wanted to give Will an out, so he didn't feel obliged to come with me. I just didn't mean to say it like that. But I felt a little better at the hurt on his face as I left him in the bathroom.

And then two-point-five seconds later, I felt a hundred times worse.

Fuck.

The next hour waiting for our lunch break was hell. The silence from Will was deafening, the clock ticked too fucking loud, and every time Will's phone buzzed with a message, my stomach twisted into knots. The second the clock ticked over to one o'clock, I was up and out of my chair.

I wasn't hungry. But I had to leave.

"Mark?" Will called out.

I turned around to face him. "You know what?" I said. "If you want to believe him over me, then that's your choice. I can't change that."

"Mark," Will said. He stood up and took a step closer to me. "Why does me being with him mean losing you?"

"Why do you believe him and not me?" I shot back at him.

"He's not like that. He's really kind of perfect, actually," Will said. "He's sweet, romantic, and charming."

"I wouldn't make this shit up. I wouldn't lie to you about something so serious."

"You have no proof," he said quietly. "Just hearsay from a barman, who Clay probably turned down. Why are you trying to ruin this for me?"

Other people in the office were looking at us, and I didn't give a fuck. "I'm trying to help you, Will. But you want proof? Fine. I'll get you proof."

I stormed out of the office, and too fucking angry to wait for the elevator, I took the stairs. I needed to find some evidence that Mr Perfect was actually Mr Asshole, and so I started at the beginning.

I needed to speak to Pete.

———

I DIDN'T EVEN KNOW if Kings would be open at one o'clock in the afternoon, but the sign on the door said it was, so I took a moment to catch my breath before walking in.

I'd never noticed the stale stench of the place before. Or how dingy it looked in the daylight. I guess I'd never been there in the cold, sober light of day before. The floor wasn't exactly clean, the furniture was discolored, and the disheveled patrons looked like they fit in. Jesus, nighttime, a dozen drinks, and neon lighting had a lot to answer for.

But I was in luck.

A guy walked into the bar from the back storeroom carrying a large box, and when he put it on the counter, I saw it was Pete.

He looked at me, and then looked again. "Mark?"

"Yeah, hey, Pete," I answered.

"You're a little overdressed," he said with a smile.

I looked down at my suit and tie. "Yeah, corporate armor."

He smiled. "What can I do for you?"

"Something you said the other night," I started. "I wanted to ask you about that Clay Damon guy."

Pete nodded as though he presumed as much. "You left in a bit of a hurry the other night."

"Is it true?" I asked. "Because I told Will and he doesn't believe me."

"I wasn't here the night it happened, but the staff talked about it," he said. "We don't have a lot of trouble here, so the few instances we have kinda stick out. That's why I remember the guy's name. Everyone thought he was the catch of a lifetime, but yeah, he really isn't."

I nodded and told him what I already knew. "The guys on the door said they knew it was a fireman who bashed his boyfriend."

Pete sighed and kind of shrugged. "Apparently someone hit on the boyfriend, danced with him or something. He took his boyfriend into the bathroom. They said the kid looked fucking scared, like he knew he was gonna cop it."

"What did he do?"

Pete shrugged. "Don't really know. The kid said he had

too much to drink and fell over, cracked his eye open on a table or something. But there were two guys who heard the whole thing and told the manager."

My stomach turned. "Who was it?" I asked. "The kid? The boyfriend? Do you know his name?"

Pete had to think for a second. "You know that Sebastian guy? Blond hair, nose ring."

"Sebastian? Works at Starbucks and comes in with red-headed Colin? *That* Sebastian?"

"Yeah, that's him."

I knew him. I'd seen him around a lot, either at the club or working at the coffee shop I refused to go into. I think I might have talked to him a few times. He was maybe a few years younger than me, rather twinky, a little bit punkish, very pretty-looking guy.

I had to find him. I didn't even know if he still worked at Starbucks. From memory, he was studying at college, so maybe he was finished studying and worked somewhere else. Maybe I'd never find him. Maybe I'd never get the proof I needed.

But I had to try.

I had twenty minutes to get back to work, so I took a detour past the coffee shop. He wasn't behind the counter, but I stood in line and ordered a coffee and a savory muffin and when the girl behind the counter asked if I wanted anything else, I gave her a smile. The type of smile that normally got me what I wanted.

"Does Sebastian still work here?" I asked. "I haven't seen him around much."

She called out to someone else. "What time does Seb start?"

"Afternoon shift," came the reply.

The girl handed me my coffee and muffin. "He'll start at four."

I gave her an appreciative smile. "Thanks."

When I got back to work, Will was already there. He looked at the Starbucks cup in my hand and frowned. He knew I didn't really like Starbucks, that I preferred smaller, more personal coffee shops—I'd complained about it enough and never let him drink there—so he was probably wondering why I'd gone there. But he never said anything. And neither did I.

Will had an onsite appointment in the afternoon, which wasn't too uncommon. Someone somewhere needed an engineer in the form of a suit to run through some numbers.

So at five o'clock, I left the office and headed straight to find Sebastian.

I saw him as soon as I walked in. He was on barista duty, working the machine, so I bypassed the line up at the counter and walked over to the end of the counter, where Sebastian was.

He looked up, and a flash of recognition flickered in his eyes. He definitely recognized me, but in case he didn't know my name, I told him.

"My name's Mark."

"Hey," he said, looking at me, then to the cup in his hand, back to me, and then to the lineup of people at the counter. "If you want coffee..."

"No, I wanted to talk to you, actually."

"Oh," he said, blinking in surprise. "What about?"

"I was hoping you could tell me something about Clay Damon."

His jaw tightened and his nostrils flared. Sebastian didn't even have to answer with words. His immediate reaction said all I needed to know.

I nodded at his silent admission. "You don't have to tell me," I said softly. "But there's someone else you need to talk to for me, if that's okay. I can bring him in here, and maybe you could take a break and speak to him."

The frothing milk in his hand seemed forgotten. "Is he seeing him?"

I nodded. "For about three weeks. Says he's perfect but I was warned. He won't believe me."

Sebastian nodded, and after blinking a few times, he concentrated on his work for a while, filling some cups. I wondered if he said all he was going to say. I would imagine it wasn't something he wanted to revisit often. He blinked again. "I'll talk to him," he said quietly.

"When do you work next?"

"Tomorrow at four."

"Can I bring him here just after five?" I asked him quietly. "Or somewhere else?"

"Here's okay," he said softly. "I'll take a break and can speak to him."

I looked at him, right in his eyes. "Thank you."

He nodded, as though he understood.

I guessed he did.

I had no clue how Will would react. I had no idea.

I just hoped he'd listen.

As much as I wanted my friend back, I just wanted him to be safe even more.

When I got to work the next day, Will was already there. I put my keys and phone in my desk drawer and stood at the end of cubicle wall that divided us. I waited for him to look at me. "After work today, would you go somewhere with me?"

Will looked at me for a long moment. I don't know what

he saw on my face or whether it the quiet desperation of my voice. "Okay."

"Thank you."

At five o'clock, I walked up the sidewalk with Will. Neither of us spoke—we'd hardly talked all day—but when I stopped at the Starbucks and held the door open for him, he looked at me. "What are we here for?"

"You wanted proof," I answered quietly. Will seemed frozen to the spot, unable to move, so I gave him a sad smile. "There's someone I want you to meet."

And with that, I walked inside.

I ORDERED TWO COFFEES, and we sat at table at the back of the café. I gave a nod to Sebastian, and Will looked at me, not touching his coffee. "Are we meeting someone here?" he asked.

Just then, Sebastian walked over to our table, wiping his hands on the small black apron tied around his waist.

I looked at Will. "I'm just gonna give you guys a minute," I said, standing up and taking my coffee to a different table.

I watched as Sebastian sat down, and Will still looked confused. I couldn't hear what Sebastian told him, but I watched the color drain from Will's face. At first he looked as though he might get up and leave, but he didn't. His eyes darted to mine as Sebastian spoke, but for ten minutes he sat and listened.

Sebastian stood up, and after briefly touching Will's shoulder, he walked back behind the counter. Will sat there for a moment, and then he looked at me. Before I could stand up, Will got to his feet and bolted out the door.

I stood up slowly, gave a nod of thanks to Sebastian and walked out onto the sidewalk. There was no sign of Will in either direction, and figuring he didn't exactly like me right now, I slowly walked home.

I felt like shit.

I threw my wallet, phone, and keys on the hall stand and pulled off my tie. I got changed into jeans and a tee-shirt and, not sure what I was looking for, opened the fridge when my intercom buzzed.

I pressed the button, and a very familiar voice said, "It's me."

I hit the door button and rested my forehead against the wall. I think I was starting to come down with something. I'd been feeling nauseous on and off for weeks.

I opened my front door and waited for Will. He walked straight inside to the kitchen and leaned against the counter. He stared at me with wide eyes, and he ran his hand through his hair.

I followed him and stood across the kitchen from him. I didn't care if he was about to abuse me or cry. I wouldn't have minded either, even if he ripped me a new one, it was better than his silence. "I'm sorry," I said quietly.

He swallowed hard. "Me too."

"I'm sorry you had to hear what Sebastian said."

Will shook his head. "Don't apologize."

"Do you hate me?"

Will's eyes shot to mine. "What? No! No, I could never hate you." He ran his hand through his hair again. "I should thank you."

I couldn't explain the relief that flooded through me. "I know you liked him, but Will, I had to do something. It must've been hard to hear all that, but to be honest, even if you tell me right now you're never speaking to me again, I'd do it again in a heartbeat. These last two weeks have been awful without you, and you wouldn't believe me when I told you that Clay was no good, and if he laid a hand on you... if he hurt you... I'd never forgive myself."

"I know," he whispered. "I'm sorry I didn't believe you."

"Was what Sebastian told you horrible?" I asked.

Will frowned and nodded.

I quickly stepped in front of Will and lifted his face with my hand. "Did Clay hurt you? Did he do anything..."

Will shook his head, but there was a sadness in his eyes. "No, but what that Sebastian guy said was... well, I could see what he meant. Clay was very intense about a lot of things."

"If he hurt you..." I started. I ran my hands down his face. "Then I'd have to kill him and then I'd be in jail with no lube, and you'd have to smuggle in a file in a cake and bring me porn and lube."

Will finally smiled. But it faded quickly. "I'm giving up," he said quietly.

"You're what?"

"Giving up," he said again, "on love."

"Don't say that."

"Why not? It works for you?"

"Does it?"

He nodded, but then changed the subject. "I need to call Clay. I'm supposed to be meeting him tonight." He looked at me. "I need to tell him we're through."

"Did you want me to call him?" I asked. "Because it would be my pleasure."

Will smiled again, but he shook his head. "No, just being here with you is enough." He looked up to the ceiling and exhaled through puffed cheeks, then he looked around my apartment and noticed the two new frames on the wall. "Did you get those silly paintings framed?"

"They're not silly," I said. "And of course I did."

He walked over to them and touched the glass of the red, yellow, and orange mess we made. "You really kept this?"

I joined him and pointed to the gray charcoal drawing. "This one is my favorite."

He gave me a sad smile and seemed a little lost for words. So I spoke instead. "I'm still sorry," I said putting my hand on his arm. "I wished things with Clay didn't turn out the way it did. I didn't set out to deliberately ruin things for you."

"I know that," he said. "I should have seen that, and I'm sorry."

"I just want you to be happy," I told him.

He eyes searched mine. "Do you?"

"Of course I do. You're my best friend, Will," I told him.

His brow furrowed and he looked down to the floor for a moment, then he looked up at me. "Mark, I—"

Whatever he was about to say was interrupted by his ringing cell phone. Startled, he took a step back and checked the screen on his phone. "It's Clay."

I stepped away, and Will walked down the short hall, presumably to my bedroom for some privacy. I ordered pizza while he told Clay he didn't think it was working out. He obviously wasn't happy with the news, because it was a rather long conversation.

I had to admit, standing so close to Will, touching him like that, was a little intense. Maybe it was just because I'd missed him these last few weeks, or maybe it was because of the conversation he had with Sebastian, the emotion of it all. I didn't know.

When he sat on the sofa opposite me, he threw his phone onto the coffee table and then followed with his feet. I already had my feet on the table between the two sofas so I tapped his foot with mine. "How'd he take it?"

Will sighed. "Not happy."

"You did the right thing."

"I know," he said. "He wanted to know if you had anything to do with it."

I laughed. "Did you tell him yes?"

Will shook his head; he didn't smile. "No, at first I told him I didn't think it was working out, but he didn't agree. So I told him it had something to do with meeting one of his exes who had the scars to prove it."

"Oh, man," I whispered.

Will shook his head angrily. "Jesus, Mark. That Sebastian kid was just twenty-two when he was with Clay."

Pizza arrived, and as we ate, Will told me what Sebastian had told him. How for the first few months, Clay would make you feel like you were the only person who mattered, and once he had you hooked, he thought he owned you.

"That's exactly what he's like," Will said. "Very generous—and focused. The, um—" Will hesitated, and he blushed. "—the sex was very intense."

Oh.

I shouldn't have been surprised they'd had sex, but I was. I didn't like the thought of Clay touching him like that.

"That's what really rang true," Will went on to say. "What made me know it was true was when Sebastian said it started with being *intense* in bed, then it became a little forceful."

I sat forward on the edge of the sofa. "Will, did he hurt you?" I asked again, this time softer.

"No," he repeated his earlier answer. "He was just...

intense. It's the only word I can think of to describe it." Will shook his head. "He held on a little tight, that kind of thing, stared at me while he... was inside me."

I shook my head at the absurdity of this conversation and took a deep breath. Will and I talked about a lot of things, including sex, but never detailed accounts. Not like that. "But he never hurt you?"

Will smiled at me. "That's the third time you've asked me that," he said. "No, he didn't. In fact, he treated me like I was the best thing to ever happen to him."

I frowned at that.

Then Will told me Sebastian had told him even he wasn't the first one Clay had hit. He thought things would be different with him, but after the incident at Kings where he'd ended up with cracked ribs and three stitches to his eyebrow, he left him.

"He didn't press charges?"

"That's what I asked him," Will said. "Sebastian said he just wanted it to be over. He said his parents came in with a lawyer to get him away from Clay, threatened if he didn't leave Sebastian alone, they'd press full charges and make such a media circus out of him, he'd lose his job."

"Smart parents," I said.

"He was lucky he had them," Will said in a whisper.

I knew what he meant. He meant Sebastian was lucky he had his parents' support, because Will certainly didn't. His parents didn't give a shit.

"I'd have come for you," I said.

He smiled sadly. "You did."

"And I would again," I told him, "with my kick-ass ninja skills, guns blazing." Then I added, "And a lawyer."

"Ninjas don't have guns."

"Ah, but these are special gun-toting ninjas. They're extra cool."

Will laughed, just as the intercom buzzed. His smile died right there. "Expecting anyone else?"

"No."

"You don't think it's Clay, do you?" Will asked softly.

I shrugged. "I don't know." I wasn't expecting anyone, but the thought of a pissed-off Clay being downstairs was rather appealing because I had an awful lot to say to him. Will and I both walked over to the intercom and he stood beside me as I pressed the button.

My mother's voice came through intercom, shrill and loud. "Romeo, Romeo, where for art thou, Romeo?"

I leaned my head against the wall, exhaled loudly, and pressed the button. "I hope you brought beer, Juliet."

"A sixer," she answered. "Is that enough?"

I looked at Will. He finally smiled as he held up three fingers and mouthed, "Three for me, three for you."

"Close enough." I pressed the door release button.

Will quickly took the empty pizza box off the coffee table and tidied up just as my mother got to the door.

"Hello, darling," she said, handing over the six pack of beer as she walked in. Then she spotted Will. "Oh, my sweet William," she said, giving him a kiss on both cheeks. "You're here!"

"I am," he said. "Can I get you a drink?"

"See, Mark, dear," she said, looking at me. "Will looks after me. He gets me a drink, I get you yours," she said, looking at the beers I was holding. "What's wrong with this picture?"

"You had the wrong son?" I guessed. I meant it as a joke, but she seemed to consider it.

"Well, if you two would just get married, then I'd have both of you!" she said matter-of-factly.

Will poured my mom a gin from the bottle I kept just for her, and ignoring her comment about pending nuptials, I took two beers and joined my mother on the sofa. "To what do I owe this utmost pleasure?"

"Well, I came to check on you," she said. "Ted had some work meeting, so I thought I'd pop in and see how you were. You were sad when you came for dinner the other night."

I glanced to Will—a look my mother didn't miss—and said, "I'm fine, Mom."

Her eyes darted to the kitchen where Will was. "Yes, I can see that."

I rolled my eyes, and she smiled and thanked Will as he handed her a drink.

"How're things with Ted?" I asked.

"Fabulous," she answered, smiling as she sipped her drink. "He's an insatiable flirt, and he drinks and smokes."

"Perfect catch!" Will said with a smile.

"I think so," she said, as she rummaged through her handbag for her cigarettes. "He's fun."

"Wedding bells soon?" I asked.

Mom lit her cigarette and blew smoke out across the room. "Not sure. Might date this one for a while first."

Well, shit. "It must be love."

Will laughed at us, and it was good to hear it. I'd missed the sound. Mom looked at him then and asked, "How about you, Will? What have you been up to?"

Will glanced at me, then back to Mom. "Not much," he said, apparently not wanting to explain the whole Clay ordeal. "Just work."

Mom groaned. "How is Old Man Hubbard? Still a pain in the ass?"

"He's still a pain in the ass," Will confirmed.

"You know, he's probably just sexually frustrated. He might need a good... what's that gross licking thing you gays do...?"

I sipped my beer. "Teabagging?"

Mom shook her head. "No."

I shrugged. "Rimming?"

She pointed her finger. "That's it. He might just need a good rimming."

"Mom..." I pointlessly chastised her.

She took a drag of her cigarette. "How does that story go? Old Man Hubbard went to the cupboard, to fetch poor Rover a bone. When he got there, the cupboard was bare, so Rover gave him a bone of his own."

"Mom!"

Will fell to his side and buried his face into a cushion, though I could still hear him laughing.

"Don't encourage her, Will," I said, almost begging. "For God's sake."

He sat up and looked at me, still grinning. "I love your mom."

My mother looked at me and sipped her drink. "Well, at least someone here appreciates me."

"I'm going to need more beer," I announced to no one in particular.

Then Mom spied something and pointed toward the rarely used dining table. "What's that?"

I looked at the box in question. "Oh, I forgot about that," I said. "I ordered Halloween costumes and they arrived last week."

"You didn't open it yet?" Mom asked.

I looked at Will. "Well, I wasn't sure if I was even going to do anything this year."

My mother gasped, oblivious to the frown Will gave me. "Mark Gattison! Halloween is this weekend! I raised you better than that."

"Yes, God forbid I don't dress up and ask for candy off strangers."

Ignoring my jibe at her parenting skills, Mom finished her drink. "Open the box," she demanded. "What are you going as? I want to see!"

Knowing it'd be less painful to do as she asked, I grabbed the heavy box and sat back down on the sofa, then ripped at the tape to open the box. The first thing I took out was a plastic bag with a picture of the Superman on the front. I held it up and threw it to Will, and then I pulled out the bag with my costume.

I showed Mom the picture on the front.

She squealed and clapped her hands together. "You'll be the best Wonder Woman ever."

I grinned at my mother. "I know, right?"

Will laughed again, then looked at the costume in his hand. "I thought I was the Boy Wonder."

Mom clucked her tongue. "Superheroes have to be versatile, dear."

I nodded at Will. "That's true." Then I told Mom, "Plus, Will thinks Robin's yellow cape isn't a real cape."

"Because it's yellow?" she asked Will.

He shrugged one shoulder. "I never said it wasn't a real cape. I just said it's not the *best* cape."

Mom shook her head. "I swear. Some days I could just punch your parents," she said, disgusted. She looked at me. "Who raises their kids to think that?"

"I know," I agreed. "It's not much to ask for. Food, shelter, love, and a comprehensive appreciation for the non-prejudicial diversification of superhero capes."

Mom nodded and tapped her glass to mine. "I'll drink to that."

I ripped open the costume bag and the first piece of clothing I pulled out was the blue pants with white stars on them. They weren't exactly big.

Mom eyed them cautiously. "Where will you put your junk?"

Will choked on a mouthful of beer. He really should be used to my mother by now.

Mom took the pants from me and holding them up, turned them to look at the back then the front. "Are you going to tuck?" she asked me. "There's not a great deal of room in there."

"I'm not going to tuck, Mom," I admitted. Then I pulled a gold wrist band from the costume bag. "Cool, check these out."

As I pulled out the other items in the costume, Will did the same with his. He held up his red cape. "See? Red capes are much better."

"Ooh," Mom said. "You should get those stretchy underpants all the gay porn stars are wearing these days and wear them instead of those blue Lycra-looking ones. They make all their dicks look huge."

"Because all their dicks are huge," I said. "They're called trophy briefs for a reason."

"True," Mom agreed.

"Are you going out for Halloween?" Will asked my mom.

She finished her drink and smiled. "We're having a private party," she said with a giggle. "Ted is going to be the Cookie Monster. I have his blue outfit all organized."

"Cookie Monster?" I asked. "Do I even want to know what *Sesame Street* character you're going as?"

"No, dear," she said like I was clueless. "I'm the cookie. I even bought the chocolate paint so he could—"

"Mom," I cut her off. "For the love of all things G-rated, please don't finish that sentence."

Will roared with laughter, and Mom shook her head at both of us. "Well, I best be going," she said. "Will, I'm calling a cab. How about you come with me, save you walking at this time of night."

"Okay, sounds good," he said, still smiling.

Mom stood up and while she called a cab, Will collected his costume, shoving it all back in the bag.

"You wanna do Halloween?" I asked. "It's kind of short notice and all."

He smiled and nodded. "Would love to."

I grinned back at him. "Good."

While Mom was still on the phone, he whispered, "Thank you, Mark. Not just for what happened with Sebastian, but also for tonight. It's been good having a laugh again."

"It sure has," I agreed. And when it came time to leave, Will stood at the door for a fraction of a second, then turned back to me. He stood there as if he was unsure of something, then he hugged me.

It surprised me at first, but as he pulled me against himself, I slid my arms around his waist and buried my face in his neck. It wasn't a friends' embrace. There were no pats on the back, it wasn't a quick hug. I didn't know what it was.

But he smelled so good, and he fit against me just right.

"Thank you," he whispered in my ear before pulling away. "See you at work tomorrow," he said as he walked down the hall with my mother.

I swear I could still feel the warmth of his body against mine.

I dreamed of Will that night. Which wasn't too weird in itself, I'd had plenty of dreams where he'd done something funny, but this was a sex-dream. We were in bed naked, writhing and grinding, then I was inside of him and he was breathing my name.

I woke up hard and close to coming.

I didn't even bother going into the shower. I jerked off in bed, groaning as I gripped myself, and it was the images of Will that replayed through my mind as I came.

Fuck, this was getting ridiculous. Just because I hadn't had sex in forever and Will hugged me, of course my stupid sleep-brain would make the two related. Those were dots my normal daytime-brain wouldn't join.

But I was certain of one thing. I really needed to get laid. I couldn't keep having sex dreams of my best friend. That would just make shit weird—and after everything we'd been through these last few weeks, weird was something we could do without.

I was telling Will when we first got to work how awesome the Halloween party was going to be, and he was laughing at my mother's Cookie Monster's cookie outfit and I was telling him to get fucked, when Hubbard walked past.

He stopped and stared at the both of us laughing, and huffed. "I liked it better when you two didn't get along."

I considered giving him the bird, but thought better of it and did some work instead.

The next few days were great. Will and I were back to our old selves, he never heard from Clay and we had the weekend to look forward to.

I just didn't realize how it would all turn to shit so soon.

CHAPTER TWELVE

IT NEVER FAILED to amaze me how long it took to get dressed as a woman.

Especially Wonder Woman.

But I had to admit, I fucking rocked that outfit. I had on the red and gold tight-fitting corset, blue short shorts with white stars, and red boots.

I walked out into my living room where Will was sitting and looked down to my bare thighs. "Should I wear stockings?" I asked him seriously. "Or tights? Or go au natural?"

Will raised an eyebrow at me. "Um..."

"It just might be a bit cold, that's all," I explained.

"Well, then you won't have to worry about tucking anything in."

I laughed. "Thanks."

He tilted his head. "Do you think Wonder Woman has three-day stubble?"

I scratched the scruff on my jaw. "This Wonder Woman does. She's very liberal."

He laughed. "Hairy armpits too?"

I lifted my arm to show him, yes. Then I looked at a

still-civilian-dressed-Will. "Come on, Clark Kent. Don't have all day," I told him. I pretended to flick hair off my shoulders. "I have to go put on my hair and accessorize and I expect you all Superman'd up when I come back out."

He called me an idiot, but after I was done, I walked back out to find a suited Superman putting on his red boots.

"You know," I said, looking down to my fake, plastic, not-as-good-as-his boots. "Your boots are so much better than mine. We should keep those for next year, and I can wear those when I'm Little Red Riding Hood."

Will stared at me, and his mouth kind of fell open.

"What?"

"Red Riding Hood," I said like he was a little slow.

He looked me up and down. "You look..."

"Fucking awesome," I said, flicking my now-existent long hair off my shoulders.

"How did you get that wig to stick?" he asked.

"Well, they had these prissy clippy things, but they wouldn't have worked, so I used double-sided tape."

Will burst out laughing, and I glared at him. "You men have no idea what we women go through to look like this."

"It's scary how comfortable you are dressed as a woman," he mumbled.

"Correction," I said. "Comfortable with myself to be dressed as a woman. There's a difference."

Will stood up and held out his hands. "How do I look?"

Will was tall and had a lean, athletic build. He filled that suit pretty damn well. "You look incredible," I told him honestly.

He blushed a little and mumbled, "I can't believe I'm doing this."

"You're going to be the best Superman there." I walked to the door and held it open for him.

"At least I have a cape, right?" he asked. He pressed the elevator button then he looked at me. "Why doesn't Wonder Woman have a cape?"

"Because I have these awesome gold bulletproof wrist guards and my super-cool whip thing," I said, showing him the coiled plastic rope tied to my shorts.

"Yeah, but you can't fly."

"I beg your pardon. I can so," I said seriously. "Plus, I have the coolest invisible plane, remember?"

"Oh, right."

"It's parked out front," I said as we stepped out of the elevator.

"Sure it is."

"It is! It's just invisible."

"How long is this conversation going to go for?" he asked as we walked out onto the sidewalk.

"Until you concede defeat."

"Superman never loses."

I stopped walking and patted down my red and gold corset.

"What did you forget?" Will asked.

"My kryptonite," I mumbled. "I had it here a second ago."

"Ha ha," Will said, rolling his eyes. "Very funny."

I grinned at him, and we continued talking shit the entire way to Kings. Along the way, we saw about twenty Iron Men, a few Hulks, a couple Captain Americas, and one guy who filled out the Hawkeye outfit very nicely. He even had a kids' pink plastic bow and arrow set. There were bears dressed as Teletubbies and so many zombies I thought we'd walked onto the set of "Thriller".

At the bar, we stood behind a lesbian couple dressed as Dorothy and The Wicked Witch who looked incredible.

When Pete, who was dressed as Rick Grimes from *The Walking Dead*, saw me with Will, he smiled.

"Everything okay?" he asked over the music.

I looked at Will. "Just Super." I waved my hand at Pete's outfit. "You make a pretty cool Rick."

"Thanks," he said with a smile. "Thought someone should try and keep the zombies in line tonight." Then he said, "What will it be, boys?"

I looked up at the Halloween cocktail board. "I'll have a brain hemorrhage, and a Kryptonite for my friend here, please."

"Oh shit," Will said. "Cocktails first up?"

"Why drink beer when you can have a brain hemorrhage?"

So maybe starting on cocktails wasn't my best idea, because we got pretty tipsy pretty quickly. It only took a few and I was feeling pretty damn good.

And horny.

Dancing with Will on a dance floor with a bunch of other people, all bumping and swaying, was a little too much for me. And given the size of my shorts, I needed to simmer down a bit.

I grabbed Will's hand and dragged him off the dance floor toward the bar. "Ugh, I need a drink," I told him, which was in all honesty probably the last thing I needed. Then I adjusted myself, causing Will to look at my crotch and very prominent hard-on.

"Jesus," he mumbled.

And then over his shoulder, my eyes caught something. If I thought the drink was the last thing I needed, I hadn't allowed for seeing this fucker.

Clay.

He was dressed as lame-ass Zorro and his eyes were masked, but it was definitely him. He was staring at Will.

He wasn't supposed to be in here. He was banned from coming in here. Maybe it was the disguise, maybe it was because every single person in here was in Halloween costumes, I didn't know. But Will followed my line of sight and turned around to see what, or who, I was looking at.

Clay smiled and took a step toward him, and I don't remember thinking about it, but I instinctively pulled Will back and stood between them.

"How fitting," Clay said. He looked me up and down. "You, dressed as a woman."

I didn't bother with replying to that comment. I took a step closer to him and stared that fucker straight in the eye. "You need to fuck off."

Now, here's the thing: I can't fight.

I'd always been the type to smile my way out of any indifferences. Never thrown a punch in my life. Not one. Never had to.

But Clay didn't know that.

I didn't flinch. I gave him the best Chuck Norris stare-down I could fake and told him, "If you lay one finger on him, you'll be getting it back in the mail. Do you understand?"

Clay smiled at me, but it was weak at best. His eyes darted from mine and he looked to the side of us. I hadn't even noticed Pete the barman was now beside us, and he was waving over two security guys. "You're not welcome here," Pete told him coolly. "You either leave on your own or be escorted out with your ass in a sling. You choose."

By then the two huge security guys were there and Clay was smart enough to leave. And right there, Wonder Woman and Rick Grimes defended Superman against stupid fucking Zorro. I tried to think of a joke or a punch line, because that would have made the best joke ever, but couldn't quite manage to pull it together.

Pete patted me on the back. "You okay?"

"Yeah, I'm fine," I told him. I turned to look at Will, who looked a little stunned. "You okay?" I asked him.

He nodded. "Yeah."

"You wanna leave?"

"No," he replied. He swallowed hard. "I want a drink."

Pete walked back behind the bar, like what just happened was nothing out of the ordinary, and quickly served up two beers.

I pulled a tenner from the top of my corset and handed it to him. "Thanks, man. I'll never swear at my TV when Rick Grimes does something uncool ever again."

He laughed and went back to serving other people. I handed Will his beer and noticed my hands were shaking.

"You okay?" he asked.

"No, I damn near crapped myself."

"You were pretty scary," he said with a smile.

"If he had've thrown a punch I would have run away and cried."

Will laughed and tapped his beer to mine. "Wonder Woman, you're my hero."

I drank my beer a little too quickly, and the adrenaline and the alcohol buzz were a heady combination. I was strangely still turned on, so I palmed my dick, not caring that Will saw me do it. I downed my beer in one go and had the best idea.

Which turned out to be one of the worst ideas of my life.

"Wanna have a double header?"

Will blinked at me. "A what?"

I laughed. "It's not back-to-back hockey games, Will." I grabbed his hand. "Come with me."

I led him through the crowd to the back room. It was a dimly lit 'supplies' room, but the only thing it supplied was a closed-door room for guys to fuck or give or get head.

Will stopped walking. "What are you doing?"

"Do you know how long it's been since I got any?"

He scoffed. "What? Is two weeks too long?"

"Two weeks? Try six months."

"Six months!" Will told the whole room, who had stopped what they were doing to look at us.

I looked around the room and gave a wave. That's when I saw them. The couple I was looking for.

I wasn't even sure of their names. Bill and Ben or something like that, but they were well known for their love of double-headers.

I gave them a nod and walked over. They smiled, knowing exactly what I was after, and slowly dropped to their knees. They faced each other, with their knees, thighs, and hips touching and I stood behind them with my legs spread and my hardening dick at the perfect height for the guy facing me.

The other guy, who was between me and his boyfriend, was facing Will and waved him over. I grinned at him, and then the guy on his knees facing me kissed his boyfriend while he ran his hands up my thighs.

Fuck.

This was going to be over embarrassingly quick.

Will walked hesitantly over toward us and stood, facing me, on the other side of the two guys on their knees. He shook his head a little.

"Come on," I said breathily. "I need this. *You* need this."

Then the guy facing me ran his hands over my cock and

slipped the material down, freeing my hard-on. I groaned when he leaned over his boyfriend's shoulder and took me into his mouth.

"Fuck," Will groaned.

Or maybe it was me.

The guy facing Will with his back against me pulled Will's hard cock out of his outfit and licked the tip of his dick. Will's head fell back and he moaned, and I couldn't stop running my hands over the big S on his chest.

And then it got to be too much. The guy sucking my dick sucked even harder and did something with his tongue, and I couldn't hold back any longer.

With a long moan, my eyes rolled back and I came.

"Oh, fuck," Will growled.

And then he did the darndest thing. Will reached over the two guys kneeling between us, took my face in his hands, and kissed me. Hard.

And then he came.

His tongue stopped in my mouth while he moaned and I could feel his whole body shake.

It was one of the hottest things I'd been part of.

Then Will stilled and dropped his hands from my face. He stared into my eyes for a long second, and I couldn't help myself.

I laughed.

Will took a step back, his face was pale and he shook his head. He tucked himself back into his Superman pants and started for the door. I shoved my dick back into my pants and stopped Will at the door. "Will, where're you going?"

"I can't do this," he said.

"Do what?" I asked. I waved back at the two guys still kneeling on the floor, snowballing it out. "They don't mind, believe me."

Will shook his head, pulled open the door, and disappeared into the crowd.

Fuck.

I stood there for a second, not sure what the hell just happened, and then started after him. By the time I made it out the front of the club, he was gone.

I asked some people—seemingly the entire cast of *Toy Story*—who were waiting out the front, "Did you guys see a Superman run out here?"

Buzz Lightyear answered. "Just got a cab, dude."

I hailed the next cab and jumped into the back seat. The cabbie looked at me and shook his head. "Invisible plane out of commission?"

I ignored his comment and gave him Will's address. Then I told him to hurry the fuck up and quit mocking my costume.

I threw the driver my last twenty and raced into Will's apartment block. I knocked on his door. "Will! Will!"

Nothing.

I banged on his door again. "Will?"

A neighbor the next door down opened his door. "Hey, princess! He's not interested."

"Does this look like a fucking princess outfit?" I shot back at him. "I'm Wonder-fucking-Woman!"

"It's midnight, asshole," he replied. "Keep the fucking noise down."

Will's door opened and he stuck his head out toward his neighbor. "Sorry," he said, then he looked at me.

And my heart squeezed.

His eyes were red.

"Will, what is it?" I asked softly. "What's wrong?"

He shook his head. "I can't do it anymore," he said. "I can't be your friend. I think it's best if we just... don't."

"What?" I didn't understand. "But, Will..."

"No, Mark, I can't. I can't do it."

"Do what?" I asked. "Will, I don't understand."

"That's just it, Mark. You'll never get it," he said, and his eyes welled with tears.

It just about killed me. "Will..." I shook my head again. "Please, tell me. What did I do? Was it tonight? In the back room, I'm sorry, I just thought..."

"No, you didn't," he cried, cutting me off. "Jesus Christ, Mark, you have no clue. And I realized tonight, you never will! After the whole mess with Clay I thought you might finally get it! I thought you might finally realize what this is," he said, motioning between us. "But you still don't get it!"

"Of course I do!" I said. "Will, you're my best friend!"

Will laughed, though there was no humor in it. "That it, Mark. That's just it." He shook his head again, and the fight in him was gone. His voice was just a whisper, "I'm sorry, Mark. But I'm done. Please don't call me, don't come by here. I just can't..."

And then he closed the door in my face.

I don't know how long I stood there for. I lifted my hand to knock and went to call out again, but every time I tried something stopped me.

He didn't want to be my friend anymore.

So I left. I walked home. One foot in front of the other. Numb.

I didn't understand. My chest felt all tight, like it hurt to breathe, and my stomach hurt. I was confused and achy, and I didn't know what he meant.

It took me so long to walk home, and when I got through the door, I stripped out of my stupid fucking costume and changed into sweats. I checked my phone, but there were no messages, no missed calls.

I curled up on the sofa and stared at my phone screen, wondering what on earth I could say to him, what questions I would ask, what I could tell him to make it better.

I just didn't know.

I thought—or rather, foolishly hoped—he'd call me or text me to say he didn't mean it.

But he never did.

I woke up on the sofa, stiff and sore, and when I remembered the night before, the now-familiar nausea and tight feeling in my chest returned. I couldn't stomach the idea of food and didn't feel like I could even stand.

It felt like something was wrong with me.

So I stayed lying down on the sofa. I turned on the TV so the noise drowned out my thoughts. I stared at the screen without watching any of it.

And I stayed there for hours.

I think I fell asleep at some point, and when I woke up, I still didn't move.

I got up Sunday afternoon to use the bathroom, and instead of going back to the sofa, I crawled into bed.

I spent the entire time in that in-between state of awake and asleep and when the sun came up on Monday morning, the only thing I did was call work and tell them I was sick.

In the hope that Will would call, I put my phone on the charger by my bed, rolled over, and went back to staring at the wall.

My cell phone rang, startling me. I read the screen and when it wasn't Will, I almost didn't answer.

It was Isaac.

I took the call. "Hello?"

"Mark?" he said. "Is that you?"

"Yeah," I said.

"It doesn't sound like you," he said. "What's wrong?"

"I think I'm sick."

"You sound awful."

I barely had the energy to speak, and my voice was croaky. "I feel awful." Then I noticed it was dark outside. "What day is it?" I asked him.

"It's Monday. Mark, are you sure you're okay?"

"I... I don't know."

"Carter wanted me to call you," he said. "How about I get him to call you back. He won't be too much longer."

"Thanks, Isaac," I said softly. I clicked off the call and closed my eyes.

The room was dark and I was wide awake when the phone rang again. I didn't flinch or jump at the sound. I picked up the phone and looked at the screen, pretty sure it wouldn't be Will and knowing damn well if it was my mother I had no intention of answering.

It was Carter.

"Mark, Isaac said something was wrong," he said, sounding concerned. "He said you weren't well, but you sounded wrong. What's up, Mark. Tell me."

I whispered, "I don't know."

"Are you hurt? Are you injured?"

"No," I mumbled. "Yes. I don't know. I just want to sleep all day, my chest hurts, and I can't even think of food. I don't know what's wrong with me."

"Mark..." he said with warning in his tone. "Is there someone who can come check on you?"

"If you're implying my mother, I'd rather not, thanks." My voice was barely a whisper.

"Mark, you're starting to worry me."

"I'll be okay," I said weakly. "I just feel... horrible."

"Do you want us to come visit? Where's Will?" Carter asked. "He'll come check on you."

Then surprising even myself, my eyes sprang tears and my voice croaked. "He's, um... he doesn't think we should be friends anymore." God, I sounded pathetic.

"What?"

"Do they have a one-eight-hundred number for awesome yet horribly pathetic people?"

"He doesn't think you should be friends?" Carter asked. "What the hell happened?"

"I don't know what I did. But he's had enough of me."

I could hear Carter mumbling something to Isaac, as though he was covering the mouthpiece.

"Maybe there's only so much awesome some people can take," I mumbled into the phone. Then I started to cry. "I mean, you had a limit. You left me too."

"Mark, we're coming to Hartford."

I wanted to tell him no, I'd be okay. Instead I just nodded in the dark and whispered, "Thank you."

————

I STILL HADN'T MOVED in two hours when there was a knock on my door. I rolled out of bed, dragging my covers with me, my entire body aching, and opened the door.

I didn't wait for them to come in or even say hello. I just walked to the sofa and threw myself on it.

I heard the door shut and the lights went on. Carter knelt in front of me. "Mark?"

I pulled the duvet cover from my face so I could look at him. "Thank you both for coming."

"What happened?" he asked softly.

"I think I'm getting the flu or something. Or maybe I'm dying. I don't know. I feel like I've been hit by a bus."

Carter put his hand on my forehead. "You don't feel like there's a fever. Where does it hurt?"

"My chest. My stomach." I put my hand against my heart. "It really hurts."

"Can you sit up for me?" he asked.

I moaned as I sat up, and when I saw the look of concern on Carter's face, my eyes betrayed me and filled with tears. "I'm sorry," I croaked out.

It was then I looked over at Isaac, who stood with Brady not far from the front door. "I'm sorry, Isaac. Please come in," I said, wiping my tears.

Isaac walked slowly over to my other sofa, and feeling the edge of it, he sat down. Carter spoke, making me look back at him. "What happened?"

I shrugged, and then I told them everything. From when he and Isaac left last time, with me trying to set Will up with a boyfriend, then the problems with Clay, how Will and I didn't talk much, and then how things were good again until Halloween. I told Carter and Isaac that I'd dragged Will into the back room of Kings even though he wasn't too interested, I made him do it, and then he freaked out. I told them that he told me he couldn't be my friend anymore, that he'd had enough.

"What were his words exactly?" Isaac asked.

I had to think about it, even though his words had been on replay for two days. "He said he was done. That I shouldn't call him or see him, that he couldn't do it anymore. He said he thought I'd understand after what happened with Clay, but I didn't. He said I was clueless, that I would never get it."

I pulled the blanket around me tighter, and Carter patted my knee. "Oh, Mark."

"I need to grow up," I mumbled.

"Did he say that?" Carter asked.

I shook my head. "No, he didn't. But I need to."

"Mark," Isaac said softly. "I don't really know how to say this without it being a little blunt, so I'm just going to say it." He cleared his throat and sat up a little straighter. "You know I love you, and you know Carter loves you. Well, so does Will."

I shook my head. "No, he doesn't. Not anymore."

Isaac shook his head and smiled patiently. "No, Mark. He's *in* love with you."

He's in love with you...

I blinked. "Huh?"

Isaac said it again. "He's in love with you. He was in love with you when we were here last, and I'd hazard a guess that he had been for some time."

I shook my head and looked at Carter. "No, that's not right. He couldn't have been."

Carter smiled at me and patted my knee before he stood up and sat back down next to me. "Mark, I know it's not something you're very familiar with, but do you think there's a possibility that you're in love with him too?"

I stared at him, then at Isaac, then back to Carter. I shook my head again. "No, he's my best friend. I mean, I love him like a best friend."

"I know you do," Carter said. "And you'd do anything for him."

"I would," I agreed.

"And you feel sick at the thought of losing him, and your heart feels like it's made of lead and you can't breathe, and you just want to see him one more time to tell him something, anything, to get him to stay."

I nodded and swallowed thickly. "Yes."

"Mark," Carter said, putting his hand to the side of my face. "You love him."

I couldn't stop the tears this time. "I don't think I know what that is," I mumbled.

Isaac frowned. He held out his hand to me, which I took, and sliding slowly off the sofa, he knelt in front of me. He put his hands to my face and wiped away my tears. "Yes you do, Mark," he whispered. "You know what love is. You have so much love in you. You're the best friend anyone could ask for. You'd do anything, give anything, without question." He ran his hands over my eyebrows and along my cheeks and into my hair. Then he rested his hand against my face. "You know how to love. You do it exceptionally well."

"And you think Will loves me?" I asked.

Isaac nodded. "I know he does. The way he was around you. What he said, how he said it, what he didn't say. It's all there, you just need to look with your heart, not your eyes."

Carter said, "Mark, do you want to see him?"

I nodded. "Really badly."

Isaac smiled. "Can I make a suggestion?"

"Sure."

"Please shower first. Because you stink."

I smiled through my tears. "Thanks."

"That's okay," he said. "Just out of curiosity, how long since you showered?"

Carter laughed this time, and even I chuckled. "Since Saturday."

Isaac sat back on his haunches, leaning away from me. "That'd do it."

I looked at my watch. "It's too late to go see him now."

"It's not too late to shower," Isaac said. "Then we can talk about what you're going to do."

"What do you mean?"

"What you're going to tell him."

I shook my head. "He said he doesn't want to see me."

"You need to get him to listen," Carter said. "And you need to tell him how you feel."

"But you could shower first," Isaac said.

"Okay, I get the point," I told him.

"Did you go to work today?" Carter asked.

"No," I told him. "I was dying this morning, under my covers."

"When did you eat last?" he asked.

I had to think about that. "I can't remember. Saturday, I think."

"You go get cleaned up," he said. "I'll order some dinner and we can talk, okay?"

I nodded and peeled myself out of my bedcovers. "Thank you, both of you, for coming. I don't really have anyone else. I have other friends I can have a drink with or a laugh with, but no one I can call... except for Will, and I don't really have him anymore."

I did feel a bit better after getting a shower and brushing my teeth, and I felt even better after I ate something. And having Carter and Isaac there, even if they had to drive for two hours and take a day off work to go home, I appreciated it more than they could know.

And I felt better after talking to them about what I had to say to Will tomorrow. I had it all planned. I'd talk to him before work or at work or at lunch or after work, and I'd tell him. I'd tell him everything, and then he couldn't be mad at me anymore, and maybe, just maybe, he might smile and make a joke about how stupid I was or how at least he'd listen to what I had to say.

Except when I got to work the next day, I waited out in front with Carter and Isaac before their planned drive back to Boston. But Will never showed.

I saw one of the girls on our floor coming out of the building and stopped her. "Hey, is Will upstairs already?"

"Oh," she said. "Didn't you hear? He resigned. Came in and saw Hubbard yesterday and left. He doesn't work here anymore."

And then that heart-squeezing thing and nauseous feeling was back. Carter put his hand on my shoulder, and I looked at him. "I need to find him."

"I'll drive you to his place," he told me with a nod. Then he looked back at the doors to my office building. "Should you tell someone you're not going to work today?"

"Fuck work," I said. "I don't care about that."

"Come on," he said. "I'll drive you."

I gave him directions and tried to take deep breaths on the way there. I was nervous before, but it was excited nerves. This was almost a dread. As if I knew, deep down, it wouldn't end well.

"We'll wait here," Carter told me. "Send me a text message if we're good to go."

I tried to give him a smile as I got out of the Jeep.

"Mark," Isaac said, "tell him the truth. That's all you can do."

I gave them a nod and went into Will's apartment complex before I lost my nerve completely.

I knocked on his door. And then I knocked again. "Will? It's me. Can I talk to you please?" There was only silence, but I swear I saw shadows under the door. "Will, I don't mind talking through the door, but I don't think your neighbor two doors down likes me."

I swear I could hear him breathing on the other side of the door.

"Will," I started softly. "I need to talk to you. I have so much to say and so much to apologize for."

The door handle turned and he slowly opened the door. Stepping aside, he silently allowed me inside and waited for me to speak.

"I went to work this morning and they told me you quit," I told him. "So I came straight here. Carter and Isaac drove me. They're downstairs waiting. They drove from Boston last night because I kind of lost it and they were worried."

Will stared at me like I wasn't making any sense. So I took a deep breath and started again. "I think you might have feelings for me, and I'm sorry I never realized before. I know I've said all along I never wanted to be with anyone, and I guess I never did."

Will blinked slowly and frowned. "Is that what you came to tell me?"

I shook my head quickly. "No. What I came to tell you was that I never wanted anyone before. But then there's you, and I have all these feelings that I don't know what to do with, and I'm still getting this whole thing wrong."

Will walked over to the kitchen. "Yes, Mark, you are."

"I'm sorry," I said. "I wish I knew how to say it."

"Say what?"

It was then I looked around his apartment. It was scattered with boxes. Moving boxes. I spun to look at him. "Are you leaving?"

He nodded and spoke to the floor. "I can't stay here."

"Because of me?" I asked quietly.

He didn't answer. Instead he said, "It's too hard to stay."

I rushed over to him and made him look at me. "Don't leave," I said, almost pleading. "I'm sorry I fucked everything up so bad, but I'm trying to make it right."

Will swallowed hard. "How? Please tell me how you will do that?"

"I think I have these feelings," I told him again. I pulled at my hair. "I think it could be love. I'm not sure, to be honest. I've never really been in love before so it's hard to tell if it's love or the flu or some other thing that makes me sick and I can't breathe."

I was rambling and not making any damn sense. "Will, please. I'm not very good at saying things like this. I keep fucking it up. I'm trying to be honest."

Will walked to the middle of his half-packed-up living room. He ran his hands through his hair and then he turned to me. "Mark, you want honesty?"

I nodded, but I was suddenly not very sure I wanted to hear this at all.

"I have known you for twelve months, and I've been in love with you for just as long. I have watched you flirt with strangers and take them home instead of me, and it killed me every time."

Oh God.

"I'm sorry."

He shook his head. "I have thought you were so perfect for so long, but you're really not."

I nodded. "I know I'm not perfect."

There was so much hurt on his face. "The other night in the back room at Kings was one of the best and worst nights of my life. I've dreamed about being with you like that, for a year for fuck's sake, and it meant nothing to you. *Nothing.*"

"That's not true," I said.

"You laughed!"

"I was drunk, and it was intense, and I don't know why I laughed... I'm sorry," I said, though it sounded hugely inadequate, even to me.

Will looked to the ground and after a too-long moment, he looked at me. "Mark, I just can't do it anymore," he said.

"But, Will," I said, feeling my eyes burn. "I came here to tell you that I have these feelings that could be love, and that I want to be with you. I want to fix this."

He shook his head and looked away. "I'm sorry," he whispered.

I wiped my tears onto my suit sleeve. "Please?"

He stood, silent and not even able to look at me.

And there it was. I told him how I felt and he said no. He didn't want me. For some stupid, conceited reason, I didn't expect that. I thought... I thought if I told him...

I needed to leave. I had to get out of there, like I was drowning and needed air. I fumbled with the door, and I ran.

Carter and Isaac were still waiting. Carter was standing, leaning against his Jeep talking to Isaac, and when Carter saw me, his face dropped. I didn't need to say anything.

He simply walked around, opened his door, and got in, waiting for me. Whether he said something quietly to Isaac, I don't know, but when I got into the car, there was only silence between us.

When we'd pulled the Jeep up in front of my apartment, Carter said, "Mark, did you want us to come up?"

I shook my head. "No. I'll be okay." But then those fucking traitorous tears began again. "You guys can go. Thank you for coming anyway," I said, wiping my face with the backs of my hands. "I'll see you guys in a week and a half for your big day, and you got my message that I'm house-sitting, yes? Because I took four weeks off and I told him I loved him and he said he doesn't want me."

"Oh, Mark..." Carter said softly.

I shook my head and sucked back a shaky breath. "I'll be okay. I just need to go home and I think I'm getting the stomach flu or something because I don't feel good at all."

I started to get out of the car, and Carter stopped me. "Mark," he said. "We'll come up."

I climbed out and stood on the sidewalk. I was going to tell them they didn't have to, but a wave of nausea rolled over me. I pushed my hand against my stomach. "Actually, I think I'm going to be sick."

I bolted for the front door and took deep breaths in the elevator. I left my front door open and raced for the bathroom.

I wasn't sick, but I stood over the sink with my head down, trying to catch my breath. I loosened my tie and splashed cold water on my face, not daring to look in the mirror. When I walked back out, Carter, Isaac, and Brady were in my living room.

I mumbled something about going to lie down and didn't look to see how they reacted. And then I felt guilty for them driving all this way and not being good company. I stopped at the hallway near my bedroom door. "I'm sorry you came all this way and took time off work. I really do appreciate it," I said, though it was a whisper at best. "But I might go and wallow in my bed for the next few decades. I'll be at your wedding, though. I promise. It'll just be me. I won't bring anyone, if that's okay." Then new fucking tears fell down my cheeks.

I scrubbed at my face and looked at Carter. "Now I've got these stupid fucking tears!" I said roughly, wiping my face again.

He walked over to me and threw his arms around me. He hugged me tight and it made the whole crying thing worse.

Carter pulled back, and after wiping my face with his hands, he said, "Give me your keys and wallet. We'll stay here for a bit while you go lie down."

I nodded. I was exhausted and my chest was all tight again, and my stomach felt like there was a ball of lead in it.

Still wearing my suit pants and work shirt, I crawled into bed and pulled the covers over my head. I closed my eyes, and because my brain didn't think I'd suffered enough, I thought of Will. Every time we'd gone out together and I'd hooked up with someone else, and the look in his eyes. Or every time he'd make some comment about relationships or boyfriends and I'd laugh, telling him how stupid and unnecessary love was. He'd shake his head at me and smile, but there was an underlying sadness there, and it was only now that I could see it for what it was.

All those months, all those times, I'd hurt him because I'd been too selfish to realize.

I'd had no fucking clue.

And now it was too late—too little, too late—and I couldn't blame him for saying no.

I should have wanted better things for him. If I really did love him, if that's what this was, then I should be happy he said no. He deserved someone that would treat him better.

So there under my blankets, I saw dozens of mental images of the hurt on Will's face over the last twelve months, each memory stabbing me with a bewildering sense of 'What the fuck have I done?'.

After a while, I heard my door open and then the bed dipped as someone sat down. I didn't bother looking. A hand rubbed my leg, and I heard Carter's voice. "Mark, you okay?"

"Mm mm," I mumbled.

"Can you come out of the blankets, please?"

"No," I croaked.

"What did he say?"

"That he couldn't do it anymore."

"Did you tell him how you felt?"

I nodded, then realized he wouldn't have been able to see. "Yeah. Well, I tried, and it was a jumbled mess at first, but in the end I think I told him."

Carter was silent for a second, so I threw back the covers to look at him. "He was supposed to say it back. In my head, that's how it was supposed to go. He was supposed to tell me he loved me back."

"Oh, Mark," he said. "I'm sorry."

"You told me to tell him," I said petulantly. "You said it would work out."

"I thought it would," he said quietly, now looking at his hands in his lap. "Mark, I really do believe he loves you."

"Well, maybe he did, but he doesn't anymore," I said, pulling the covers back over my head. "He said he did," I added from under my covers. "But it was past tense."

"What else did he say?"

"Not much," I said with a shrug. Then I pulled the covers down again. "There were boxes. Packing boxes. Like he was moving."

Carter's eyes widened. "Did he say where he was going?"

I shook my head. "I didn't ask. I just asked him not to leave. I fucking begged him. I wanted to work things out, but he said he couldn't do it again."

I rolled over onto my side and brought my knees up.

"He even quit his job to get away from me, Carter," I mumbled. "God, he really must have had enough of me."

"Did you want to try texting him?" Carter asked. "Or calling him?"

"No," I whispered. "Maybe later. Maybe never. I don't know." Then I remembered. "He doesn't want me to call him."

He patted my leg. "Just let me know if you need anything."

"It hurts, Car," I whispered and fresh tears welled in my eyes.

He leaned down and kissed my head. "I know."

I must have fallen asleep at some point, because when I pulled back the covers the light had changed in the room. Without looking at the time, I'd guess it was afternoon.

I could hear voices and at first I thought it was the TV, but then I remembered Carter and Isaac were here. I considered getting up, but thought better of it, and it wasn't long after that when my door opened.

This time it was Isaac.

He was carrying a tray with a plate and a cup on it. "I'm sorry, room service. You're cute and all," I said. My voice was croaky. "But I think you might have the wrong room."

He smiled as he edged his way into the room. "Help a guy out here," he said.

I threw back the covers and rolled out of bed. I gently took the tray from him, putting it on my bedside table, and led him to the bed, where he sat down.

I climbed back into bed and pulled the covers over my legs, though this time I stayed sitting up.

Isaac reached out, so I gave him my hand. "You've had a rough few days, huh?" he asked.

I nodded. "Yeah. Not my finest."

I noticed the house was quiet. "Where's Carter?"

"Oh, he's taken Brady out for a pee and to fill the Jeep with gas. We'll need to leave soon."

I nodded again. "I really do appreciate you being here, Isaac. I know I've been wallowing. I'm sorry."

"You're allowed to wallow." Then he said, "I'm sorry if I misled you. I told you Will was in love with you."

"You weren't wrong," I told him. "I just blew it, that's all."

Isaac was quiet for a moment, as he traced my fingers with his own. "For what it's worth, I think you did the right thing."

I didn't quite get how having my heart torn to shreds was the right thing, so I gave him time to explain.

"It's better that he knows how you feel," Isaac said. "You won't have to wonder what if, you know? It's better that you don't leave things to chance."

"Maybe," I said. "It just doesn't feel like it right now."

Isaac smiled sadly, then he took off his glasses and let his hands fall to his lap. It was only the second or third time I'd seen him without them. "Do you remember in Boston when you took me to buy my and Carter's rings? It was a surprise, remember?"

"Yes, I remember," I said. It was the day he asked Carter to marry him. How could I ever forget?

"I was unsure if the ring should have been a commitment ring or an engagement ring, but you didn't hesitate," he said with a fond smile. "You said not to waste a day, remember? I was scared he'd say no, considering what I'd put him through, but you told me if he said no today, just to ask him again tomorrow. And the day after that, and the day after that."

I nodded. "But he said yes."

Isaac smiled widely. "And I'll be forever grateful that he did. But do you get my point?"

"You want me to ask Will to marry me?" I asked incredulously. "He won't even look at me!"

Isaac chuckled and shook his head. "No. But you took a chance, for the first time in your life you told someone you loved them."

"Yeah, and I'm now reminded why that was a bad idea."

"It wasn't a bad idea, Mark." Isaac gave me a half smile. "So tell him again tomorrow and the day after that and the day after that."

"I don't mean to be ungrateful for the advice, Isaac, I seem to remember a certain someone fucking things up royally with Carter not too long ago."

Isaac smiled. "I did. And I learned from that. I'll do whatever it takes to make him happy, Mark."

"The only thing that would make Will happy right now is my absence."

Isaac turned his face toward me. "Give him time. You'll see."

He seemed so sure. "How do you know?" I asked.

"Because the last time we were here and we went to the Oak Hill open day, Will was so smitten with you. The way he talked about you..."

I frowned and as I thought of all the horrible things I'd said to him since then, another wave of nausea rolled over me. I lay back down on the bed and groaned. "Ugh, I feel awful. I think I'm getting sick."

Isaac squeezed my hand. "It's called a broken heart, Mark."

"It's horrible," I said softly.

"It's the very worst."

"Then why do we do it?" I asked. "Why do we bother with love if it feels like this?"

"Because as bad as you feel right now, love is a million times better."

I pulled the blanket over my head again. "That's bullshit."

Isaac chuckled. "Eat something, please," he said. Then the bed dipped as he got up and I heard the door close behind him.

I tried to picture eating the sandwich and juice on the tray he brought in, but the thought made my stomach lurch. I rolled over and stayed in my cocoon of wallowing, thinking about what Isaac had said.

———

I HEARD Carter's voice mumble something out in the living room, and a moment later, the bed dipped by my side.

I didn't bother pulling the covers down. "I get it now," I told him quietly. "I understand. I always thought you and Isaac were crazy for going to therapy. I always thought if love was hard, then it wasn't worth it. But I get it now. I understand what Isaac was telling me. Because I'd do anything for Will."

"Anything?"

I was expecting Carter's voice, but I was wrong.

It was Will's.

CHAPTER THIRTEEN

I BOLTED upright and pulled the blanket off my head. "Will?"

He was sitting on my bed right next to me. I think he was trying not to smile. "Were you really hiding under your blankets?"

"It's my cocoon of self-pity."

Will smiled and looked down at his hands. "Carter came to see me," he said.

I looked to the open door where Carter stood. He smiled at me, and I looked back at Will, a little stunned. "Really? I thought he went to get gas." I looked back to Carter. "I thought you went to get gas."

"You wouldn't get out of bed," Carter said. "I had to do something."

I looked back at Will, excited that he was here, but nervous too. He looked at me too, and for a long moment, neither of us spoke. Then he looked down at his hands again. "Can we talk?"

I nodded, but before I could say anything, Carter

walked into the room. "Mark, we have to get going. We need to get home."

I tried to get up, but was tangled in sheets and blankets and I almost fell off the bed. Carter bit back a grin. "Don't get up."

I kicked my leg until I was free of my covers. "I'll walk you out," I told him. I looked back at Will. "You'll stay while I say goodbye to them?"

"Of course," he said.

We walked out to the living room, where I hugged Isaac, then Carter. "Thank you both for everything."

Carter hugged me again and whispered in my ear. "You'll be okay."

I pulled back and nodded. I gave Brady a big hug and told him to look after Isaac, and with promises to call them later that night, I thanked them again and told them I'd see them in Boston in a week and a bit.

Then Carter looked at Will. He smiled and extended his hand, which Will shook. With a nod, something unsaid passed between them, and then Carter and Isaac left.

And then it was just me and Will.

I looked around my apartment, realizing that Carter and Isaac must have tidied up for me, and then I looked down at myself. I was still wearing my suit pants and shirt, which were now creased, and I was still wearing socks. I don't even remember taking my shoes off. I tried patting my down my hair. "God, I'm a mess."

We both stood in my living room, neither of us sure what to say. So I figured I'd start. "Will, I'm sorry," I said.

He stared straight at me. "Is what you said earlier true?"

With my heart in my throat, I nodded. "Yes."

"All of it?"

I nodded again. "Even the rambling bits that made no sense."

Will smiled at that. "I always understand your ramblings."

"I know you do. You're the only one who ever did. I used to confuse Carter."

Will's lips twisted in a bit of a smile. "He came to see me," he said again. "Carter did. He said he thought I should know that you weren't coping very well."

I shrugged. "I, um... yeah, that's probably true."

"He said you thought you were having heart problems, cardio-something."

"Cardiomyopathy," I corrected him. I put my hand over my heart. "I'm still not sure it's right. It kind of hurts to breathe, and it made me feel sick."

Will was smiling now.

"It wasn't funny," I told him. "I thought I was dying."

He took a few slow steps toward me. "Did you really hide under your blankets?"

"See, there's no way I can answer that without losing some manly credibility," I said.

He took another step closer. "He said he was worried about you. That's why he and Isaac drove from Boston. He said he spoke to you on the phone and you sounded awful."

"I thought I was dying," I said again, though it was softer this time. "I thought I'd lost you and it... almost killed me."

Will stepped right up close so I could feel the heat of his body against mine, and my words died in my throat. His eyes were intense and my heart was hammering, and when his hand touched the side of my face, I thought my heart might burst in my chest. "So you really meant what you said before?"

I nodded quickly. "Yes." It was then I noticed he was still wearing the bracelet I bought him. I lifted my hand to his and touched the leather band. "You never took it off."

He shook his head slowly. "I couldn't."

I swallowed hard, and when he put his hand back to my face, I leaned into the palm of his hand and sighed. "Will..."

"I've waited twelve months to do this right," he whispered. Then he leaned in slowly, so his lips were almost touching mine, and then oh-so-lightly, he kissed me. My eyes fluttered closed and my breath caught and my heart just about stopped.

His lips were warm and open, and his hand slid around my jaw and he kissed me, slow and sweet. When he pulled back, it took a while for me to open my eyes, but when I did, he was smiling.

I wanted to tell him something amazing, something profound. Instead, I said, "My knees feel funny."

Will laughed, and this time, I put my hands to his face and kissed him, deeper, longer. I opened his lips with my own and teased his tongue with mine. He moaned and the sound of it tightened the knots in my belly. And when the kiss simmered, I slid my arms around his waist and buried my face in his neck.

There was nothing, *nothing*, that compared to that moment.

"My God, Will," I said, breathing in his scent. My hands ran up his back and I held him tighter. "I can't believe it. I don't..." I pulled back so I could see his face. "I don't know what I'm doing. I don't know the first thing about being a boyfriend, if that's what I am, or maybe I shouldn't have said that—oh my God, is that embarrassing? Should I be embarrassed?"

Will pecked his lips to mine to shut me up. "No, it's not embarrassing. You ramble when you're nervous. It's cute."

I took a step back from him, but took his hand and led us to the sofa.

"Will, can we talk about this?" I asked. "I need to say sorry. I need to apologize for not knowing. I wish I knew. I wish I'd known twelve months ago, when we first met, that you liked me that way."

Will looked down at our joined hands. "You would have run a mile."

I shook my head quickly, then realizing he was probably right, I gave him a bit of shrug. "I'm not running now."

Will looked at me and smiled. "No, you're not." He bit his lip. "Can I ask you something?"

"Sure."

"Is this really what you want?" he asked, looking again at our hands. "I mean, it wasn't three days ago."

"I didn't know what it was three days ago," I told him honestly. "I mean, seeing you with Clay or even with that Grant guy or Jayden fucking killed me, but I just thought I was feeling left out or something. It wasn't until you ran out of Kings and told me you didn't want to be friends anymore that I really fell apart." I shrugged. "I didn't know what it was or why I felt so bad. I told Carter my heart hurt, and that's when he and Isaac explained to me what it was and why I felt so bad."

"You had no clue?"

I shook my head. "I've never been in love before..."

Will licked his lips, the way he did when he was nervous. "And you're in love now?"

I grinned at him. "Well, it's either that or I have some rare condition that gives heart palpitations and wobbly knees when I look at you."

"Is that your cardiomyopathy?"

I nodded. "It was almost fatal. Very serious."

"Miraculous recovery," he said.

I smiled at him, but then I told him seriously, "Will, I want to make things right with you. I want this. I want there to be an *us*. I don't really know how to make that work, because I've never had to before—I've never *wanted to* before—but I want to now, and I'm sure I'll fuck something up, but you'll tell me because you've always told me when I fuck something up. And maybe that's the best part of falling in love with your best friend, because you know me so well."

"You're rambling again."

"I can't help it. I'm waiting for you to tell me no."

Will sat back on the sofa, folded one leg under the other, and turned so he faced me. "Mark, I'm not saying no. But we need to talk about this."

I nodded quickly. "I know. And I know I might not like a lot of it. If the way I felt these last few days is how you felt for most of the last year... God, all I can say is I'm sorry."

"You didn't know. I don't blame you for that," he said. "But I went on those dates with other guys to see if you'd care enough to stop me."

"I didn't know why I was so jealous," I told him. "I know that sounds stupid. How could I not know?" I asked rhetorically. "And maybe I've felt something for a while. I've not been with anyone for a long while. I just haven't been interested. And then the other night in the back room of the club. God, you have no idea how sorry I am about that."

Will gave me a sad smile. "That was the last straw for me," he said quietly. "To watch you... like that..."— he dropped to a whisper—"when you came"—he shivered —"and it was like some game to you."

I shook my head. "It wasn't a game. My head had been all over the place and it'd been so long since... well, it'd been six months since I'd had any kind of encounter with someone and then finally getting you back in my life and too many drinks and then getting to tell Clay I'd cheerfully cut his hands off, well, it was all just too much. I needed some kind of... release. And I'm really sorry."

"Don't apologize," he said quietly. "We can't change what happened."

"I'm still sorry," I told him. "And like I said before, I know what it means now. When people say they'd do anything for the people they care about, I know what that means. I used to think Carter and Isaac were crazy going through everything they went through, I mean, they went through hell and are now happily going through couples therapy to make things right. But I get it now. Will, I'd do anything to make things right with you."

Will's lip curled in a half smile. "Well, I don't think we need couples therapy. Yet. I mean, when we spend two days arguing about things like superhero capes, we might want to reconsider."

I played with his fingers, and when I looked at him I couldn't help but smile. "Can I kiss you again? Because that kiss before was pretty damn amazing."

He grinned at me and leaned in, so leaving his hands on his leg, I cupped his face and softly pressed my lips to his. I teased his lips with mine, barely kissing him, and his scent still filled my head. I kissed him a little harder then, slowly tasting his tongue. Will touched my arm, my neck, then my face and we kissed until my head spun.

I pulled my mouth from his to take in some air, and keeping my forehead pressed to his, I said, "Jesus, Will."

He smiled and licked his wet lips. "I've dreamed of

kissing you, of holding hands with you for the longest time," he whispered. He closed his eyes. "I tried to move on, but I couldn't. I didn't know what else to do. I quit my job, Mark. I gave notice on my place."

"You were really leaving?" I asked. Then it occurred to me. *Oh fuck.* "Are you still leaving?"

Will looked at me for a long moment. "I was. I really was going. Now I don't know what I'm doing."

"You're staying here," I told him. "I don't just mean Hartford, I mean here, in my apartment. Just for the next week or so. Then I have four weeks off in Boston, house-sitting for Carter and Isaac. You can stay with me there. We'll walk Missy, Carter's dog, and the cat hates me but he might like you, and we can sleep in and swim and look around the city."

"You put in for vacation time when I was with Clay," he said quietly. It wasn't a question.

I nodded. "Yeah, I did. I couldn't stand to watch you be so happy with him. It was killing me, but I didn't know why. I thought you could do without me for a while."

Will sighed deeply. "It was a pretty fucked-up couple of weeks, wasn't it? With us not talking and that."

"It was horrible," I agreed, remembering how I'd felt without him. "I can't believe you were really going to leave."

"Even after you came around to see me this morning and I yelled at you," he said, "I was still leaving. I thought you just didn't want to lose me as a friend, and I just couldn't go through it all again. I'd been in love with you pretty much since the day I met you, and I couldn't just be 'friends' anymore." He took my hand in both of his. "Even when you said you had feelings for me, after I'd waited so long to hear you say that, I just thought it still wasn't real. I thought if you didn't love me the day before, how could you love me now. It wasn't until Carter called around to talk to me that I believed you."

To hear him say that stung a little, but I guessed it was a fair reaction, all things considered. I still could hardly believe Carter went to see him. "What did Carter say?"

Will smiled at me. "I told him that I didn't see what could change in a day to make you love me now when you didn't the day before. And he said everything had changed.

"He said everything *for you* had changed. He said you realized that what you thought was just a friendship was really something more, but you just wouldn't admit it," Will said. "Then he reminded me that you'd never really been in love before, and that I knew you better than anyone, himself included. He asked me if I honestly thought you would lie about that, and I knew you wouldn't. Carter told me he's known you for years, and he didn't think he'd ever see the day when you would be in love." Then Will chuckled, "He thought you were in love with me when he and Isaac visited last time, but he said it was Isaac who picked up on it first. Apparently your voice changes when you talk to me. I'm not sure how that works, but that's what he said."

"My voice changes?"

"Yep, you can add that to your cardio problems, knee problems—"

I finished for him. "Head-spinning problems, tummy butterflies, nausea, not being able to eat, and now voice-changing problems? Jeez, this whole romance thing is bad for your health."

Will laughed and shook his head at me. "I still can't believe you thought you were dying. I think you could add hypochondriac to that list."

"I had a cocoon on my bed from two days of wallowing, but Isaac made me wash it. Apparently it stunk."

Then Will leaned back on the sofa and let his head fall back with a sigh. "I still have two weeks on the lease on my place, so I don't need anywhere to stay right now," he said. I couldn't help but feel a little disappointed, even though I knew him living here was ludicrous considering we'd only technically been together for about twenty minutes.

I think Will liked my disappointment, because he smiled when he said, "But I could come to Boston."

"Really?" I asked with a ridiculous grin. "You'll come? It'll be so much fun. Just us for four weeks." Then I remembered something. "Oh, the wedding... Will you come to that too, please? Please say you'll come to that."

Will grinned at me, the kind where his eyes crinkled at the sides. "You're really excited, aren't you?"

I bounced a little in my seat. "I am. I'm kind of so happy it's absurd." And then I laughed at myself and I could feel my cheeks heat with embarrassment.

Will's hand came up and touched the warmth on my face, and he stared at me for a long moment. "You're really here, aren't you?" he whispered. "With me."

I smiled into the palm of his hand. "I really am."

Just when I thought it was pretty fucking perfect, Will said, "Mark, I don't think we should have sex."

Slowly, I sat up straight and looked at him. "Well, that was random, but okay, if that's what you want."

He blushed this time. "I mean, I want to have sex with you, I *really* do, but I think we should wait," he clarified.

"Oh."

"I just don't think we should rush into anything," he said quickly. "I just think if we start having sex, we won't stop, and I want us to talk first. I think we need to talk about stuff, and I know that sounds mushy and shit, but I don't want to fuck this up just because we fell into bed too soon."

I leaned in and planted a kiss right on his lips. "Now it's you that's rambling," I told him. "And it's fine with me. Whatever you want, Will. I think it's a good idea, actually, because yeah, I'm sure you're right about the sex thing."

Will's eyes shone when he smiled. "Are you sure you're okay with that?"

"I am," I told him honestly. "But just so we're clear, how long are we talking?"

Will laughed at me, but then he leaned in and whispered in my ear, "I think we'll know."

Then, ruining the best moment of my life, my stomach growled. Will smiled at me. "Someone's hungry."

"Someone has eaten hardly anything these last few days."

Will touched my face and sighed. "Oh, that's right. You were dying."

"I was," I said with a smile. "Completely terminal."

"Oh really? But you're better now. What fixed it?"

"You," I answered quickly. "But we better order a pizza just in case."

"Yes, we better. God forbid you need to hide under your blankets in your work clothes again."

I looked down at my suit pants. "I went to work and they told me you quit," I said. "So I left. Actually, I never even got through the doors. I called in sick yesterday, because I couldn't get out of bed, and then I was a no-show today. Hubbard will probably fire me tomorrow."

Will smiled. "He was rather disappointed it was me quitting and not you."

I snorted. "So, just out of curiosity, when Hubbard calls me into his office tomorrow—and we know he's going to— what do I tell him?"

"Tell him you needed to sort things out with your boyfriend."

Boyfriend.

"Really?"

Will nodded and grinned. "Yep." Then he leaned in and kissed my smiling lips.

Only this time, we kissed a little harder, a little deeper, and we held on a little tighter. Fuck, he was like crack. I couldn't get enough. I slid my hand through his hair so I could hold his face to mine, and he groaned into my mouth.

Will ran his hands around my back, pulling us impossibly closer, and this kiss became more than just a kiss. It was like we were trying to crawl into each other.

I wanted him. I'd never wanted anything more in my entire life.

And his hands moved to my face, and he pulled his lips from mine. He kept our faces together but we were breathing heavily and Will's eyes were closed.

"Holy shit, Mark," he whispered. "We should stop."

I nodded.

"Is that okay?" he asked. "If we stop, I mean. Are we good?"

I smiled and kissed him softly this time. "We are so fucking good."

Will laughed, then he pulled back and finally opened his eyes. He seemed as dazed as I was. He exhaled loudly and said, "How about we order that pizza?"

CHAPTER FOURTEEN

THE TRIP to Boston from Hartford was normally a fairly boring two hours, but this time I rode shotgun while Will drove.

I sat with my hand on his thigh and smiled pretty much the whole way there.

Actually, I don't think I'd stopped smiling for eight days.

It turns out I was one of those types of people most other miserable single people hated. Like one of those in-love people who I used to make fun of. Yep, one of those. I was all over Will, I had to touch him, kiss him, all the time. Even looking at him would make me smile.

My past-me really would've hated present-me.

But I loved it.

I wondered how I'd gone twenty-seven years without it.

We'd spent the last eight days talking and taking things slow like we said we would. We made out a lot, and every day after work as soon as he was through my front door, I was all over him. And after we'd spend the better part of an hour making out—in the kitchen, on the couch, on the floor —we'd have dinner and spend hours talking.

It was kind of perfect.

I didn't even mind the no-sex rule. I understood his reasoning for not wanting to jump into bed so soon, and I really did agree with it. We needed to be on solid ground first, even if it made for some uncomfortable dinners and long solitary showers.

It was making us stronger. And I was all for that.

I was used to seeing him at work every day, so it was weird going to work and not having Will there. Hubbard had replaced him with someone who just didn't even come close. I'd told Will that I'd met his replacement, and he still laughed when he thought of it. Two days ago, Hubbard had found me threatening the photocopier and stood in the doorway with a woman who smiled cheerfully at me. I could tell he was hesitant in even introducing us. "Here you are, Gattison," he said. "I was going to show Rebecca the photocopy room."

So, me being me, I waved my hand in front of myself and said, "These are not the droids you're looking for."

Will had laughed. "How did he take that?"

"You know those cartoons when steam comes out of the little short, bald guy's ears?"

"Yeah."

"Well, he looked just like that."

Will cracked up laughing. "What did the new girl do?"

I shrugged. "I don't know. She didn't get the reference to the droids and I told Hubbard I couldn't work with anyone who didn't get *Star Wars* references."

"I bet he would have loved that."

"He told me I was the reason he needed blood pressure medication," I said.

Yep, Will still chuckled to himself when he remembered it. Hubbard had also told me to use this four weeks' vacation time to decide if I wanted to be a part of his team or not. I figured I'd save him some blood pressure meds and tell him I planned to do exactly that.

The truth was, I didn't know what I wanted.

All I knew was that it would involve Will.

A few months ago, I was obliviously happy in my little bubble. Then it fell to shit but now it was better than it had ever been.

I gave Will directions to Carter and Isaac's and I couldn't help but smile as we pulled into their street. And when we pulled up in the drive, Will stared at me.

"What?" I asked.

"You haven't stopped smiling yet."

"I know. It's ridiculous."

"It's very cute," Will said with a smile.

I leaned over the console and kissed him quickly. "I'm really looking forward to this," I told him.

"The wedding or the month house-sitting?"

"Both. Come on, let's get in there. Isaac probably has Carter stressed over wedding plans," I said, getting out of the car. I grabbed the two tailored suit bags that were hanging up in the backseat. Will grabbed the two suitcases.

Will looked back at the house, and I could tell he was a little surprised at just how nice it was. "Nice, huh?"

Will nodded. "And we're staying here for a month?"

I pressed the doorbell. "Yep."

The door swung open and Carter grinned when he saw us. "Hey!" He quickly threw his arms open and hugged me tight. "Well, you look better than the last time I saw you," he said.

I pulled back and gave a pointed nod to Will. "He might have something to do with that."

Before Will could blush properly, Carter hugged him

too. It sounded like he whispered, "Thank you," but I couldn't be sure.

Isaac appeared in the door. He was smiling. "There sounds like an awful lot of happy out here."

"Hey you," I said. I touched his arm first, then hugged him. And for good measure, I kissed his cheek. "I owe you and Carter a very big thank you."

"No you don't," Isaac said kindly. "You were there for Carter when he needed someone, and it was only right that we returned the favor. But please tell me you're not here alone."

I laughed. He knew damn well I wasn't. "Will's being mauled by Carter."

"Mark overexaggerates," Will said.

Isaac turned his face to the sound of Will's voice. "I'm really glad you're here, Will," he said. "Please come in."

We walked inside and Carter, who was now carrying one of the suitcases, said, "I'll put you guys in the second bedroom."

I was going to tell him that we'd prefer separate rooms, but before I could answer, Will said, "No problem."

I wasn't adverse to this, hell the fuck no, but it was going to make the no-sex-yet rule all the more difficult. But we dropped our stuff onto the queen-sized bed and quickly made our way out to the kitchen.

We were greeted by Brady and Missy and promptly ignored by the cat. Isaac poured us an iced tea, and we told them about the last eight days. We told them about my job dilemmas, how Will was considering going back to college.

"Really?" Carter asked. "University?"

Will smiled. "Yep. I want to further my engineering degree, and perhaps major in civil engineering rather than just tension cables."

"You know," Isaac said. "Boston has some great colleges."

I laughed. "Be careful what you wish for," I told them. "We're not sure where we want to go." I rubbed my thumb on Will's arm, letting him know I was serious when I said the word 'we'.

"What about you?" Carter asked me. "If Will's going back to college, would you consider going back?"

"Pfft," I scoffed. "Good Lord, no." Then I said, "I don't know what I want to do. I don't want to stay where I am. I can't stand working for anyone, especially someone like Hubbard. I want something that's mine but something that's new..." I shrugged. "I don't know."

Carter smiled, looking between the two of us. "I'm really glad you two got everything sorted out."

I slid my arm around Will and gave him a squeeze. "So am I," I told Carter. "And I really need to thank both you and Isaac for coming to Hartford and making me see what was right in front of me."

Will ducked his head, embarrassed, but I leaned in and kissed his temple. Carter smiled warmly at us, and when I looked to Isaac he had his head tilted slightly.

"Isaac?"

"Um," he said. "Can I ask something?"

I was a little hesitant, never really knowing what could come out of his mouth. "Sure."

"We do have another bedroom," he said simply. "You don't need to feel pressured into sharing the same room."

"Huh?"

"When Carter said he'd put your bags into the same bedroom, you both paused before answering," he explained. "It's no big deal. You don't have to share a bedroom."

Carter looked at me, clearly surprised. "Shit, I'm sorry. I didn't realize, I just assumed..."

Now it was my turn to blush. "The same room is fine. I'm sure we'll manage," I said. I cleared my throat. "Thanks, Isaac, for bringing that up."

He opened his mouth, obviously going to say something, but then he smiled instead. "I wasn't judging, I was just saying we have another spare room."

Will leaned into me and said, "Um, that was my stipulation. I thought it would be best to... abstain for a while." Will looked at me, obviously embarrassed.

I smiled and kissed him. "And it's a good thing," I told them.

Carter was grinning and clearly trying not to laugh. "*You* think it's a good idea?" He shook his head. "Jesus, you do have it bad."

"Hey!" I said. "I'll have you know it's been a long time for me, and I'm more than happy to do this for us."

"How long is a 'long time' for you?" Isaac asked.

I was used to Isaac's no-boundaries personality, but I think Will was a little uncomfortable. I ran my hand up his back and leaned into him, letting him know it was okay. "It's been over six months for me," I said, smiling back at Will who was smiling at me.

Carter almost spat his drink out. "Six months!" he cried.

"It's not *that* long, and yes, it was Will's idea, but I happen to agree with it," I said. "I want to prove to him that I'm serious."

Carter walked over to Isaac and slid his arm around his shoulder. He sniffled and wiped his eye, pretending to be emotional. "Oh honey, our little boy's all grown up."

"Shut the fuck up," I told him, but I was smiling.

Will laughed and put his arms around me, kind of

shielding me from Carter and Isaac. Even though they were not a threat in the slightest, it was like Will was protecting me, and I liked it. I liked it a lot.

I peeked over his shoulder and stuck my tongue out at Carter. "Are you finished talking about my sex life?"

Carter snorted. "Mark, I am in shock," he said. "You, of all people, with your fuck-anything-that-moves attitude has done a full one-eighty. I'm impressed." Then he clapped Will's shoulder. "I always thought it'd take someone special to tame him."

"Yeah, well," I said, stepping around Will but tucking myself into his side. "You can stop picking on me anytime now. I get enough of that from my mother."

"Oh my God," Carter said. "What did she say when you told her you were, you know, together?"

"Ugh," I groaned. "Don't ask."

Will chuckled and explained the story. "We'd been to see my parents first. I'd told them I'd quit my job and was spending the next four weeks here with Mark. Then I told them Mark and I were together, and well, that didn't exactly make my mother's day."

"She hates me," I told them. "I swear she thinks I turned Will into some sinning sex fiend."

"Which, as any sane person would know, is a load of crap," Will said.

"What about your dad?" Isaac asked.

"He does whatever my mother tells him to do," Will said. "Always has. I don't actually remember a time in my life when he said more than ten words at a time, so it was no great surprise he said nothing."

"I'm sorry to hear that," Isaac said softly.

Will shrugged. The indifference from his parents was nothing new to him. "Anyway, we left my parents' house," he went on to say, "and we thought we may as well get it over with with Mark's mom too."

I sighed dramatically, and Will started to smile. "Well," he said, "we walked in and Mark took my hand. He didn't even have to say a word! She just squealed and launched herself at me."

"Yeah," I added flatly. "Then she proceeded to cry about getting the son she always wanted."

Will laughed again. "She did correct herself and said she meant to say son-in-law."

"Oh please," I said. "She meant what she said all right."

Carter burst out laughing. "So I take it she's happy?"

I rolled my eyes. "Oh yes. She has the son she's always wanted now," I said sarcastically. "She hugged him for dear life and slapped me up the back of the head and told me it took me long enough."

"Well, it took you a year," Will said with an exasperated sigh.

"Right," I said, changing the subject. I pulled on his hand and led him out of the kitchen. "Come on," I said, looking back to Carter and Isaac, "enough about me. How about we show Will the house, introduce him to Missy and that evil cat of yours, then you two can tell us what we need to do for this wedding in two days."

———

I WAS nervous about getting into bed with Will, and by the way he was talking nonstop while we got ready, I assumed he was nervous too.

Stripped to just my briefs, I slid into the bed, pulled back the covers on his side, and patted the mattress. He bit his lip, climbed in, and I pulled the covers back over him.

I leaned in and sweetly kissed him. "Good night."

Then Will leaned up on his elbow, bent over me, and kissed me. His lips lingered on mine, his tongue tempted my own, but I pulled back. Dazed at the intensity of just a kiss from this man, I shook my head. "If we start..."

Will groaned. "I know."

Keeping my hand on his face, I slid my hips back, away from him. "Ugh. You're killing me."

"Do you really mind?" he asked. "You say it doesn't bother you, but it obviously does."

"If you mean 'obviously does' because of the perma-hard-on I've had since last week, then yes, it's obvious. But no, I don't mind."

"The perma-hard-on?" he asked. I could see his smile, even in the darkened room.

I nodded. "Yes. I jerk off a lot. I should consider shares in Kleenex."

Will chuckled, turning his face into the pillow to muffle the sound. "For what it's worth, it's killing me too."

I leaned in and quickly pecked my lips to his. "Good."

We talked until we fell asleep, but the second night ended a little differently. We'd spent the day doing last-minute errands for the wedding. We'd had dinner with Hannah and Carlos and the cutest kid on the planet, little Ada, and Isaac went home with them. He wanted to keep the tradition that he and Carter don't see each other before the ceremony.

Isaac had even joked that he really needn't worry about him seeing anyone before the wedding—or after that matter—but he wanted to do this right. Isaac made me swear that we'd help Carter in the morning if needed and calm him down if he looked like panicking.

We'd tidied up after dinner and crawled into bed, only

this time when I kissed him goodnight, he took my face in his hands and really kissed me.

I mean, he really fucking kissed me.

He pulled us together and then rolled on top of me. I kissed him back with equal fervor and widened my legs for him, needing him as close as possible. I found myself bucking my hips, reveling at his weight on mine.

We were both hard. I could feel his cock pressed between us as we were grinding against each other. I rolled us onto our sides and slid my hand over his ass and then beneath the elastic at the front of his briefs.

I wrapped my hand around his cock, and he soon did the same to me. No, it wasn't intercourse, but it was intimate and wonderful. To be with him like that, to hold him, to feel him.

I came first, as his hand squeezed me and his tongue invaded my mouth. Soon after, Will pulsed in my hand, shooting hot cum onto my hand and stomach.

"Fuck, Will," I murmured against his lips. "That was so hot."

He gave me a lazy grin. "Mmm."

I kissed his smiling lips, then his half-closed eyelids. "Stay here. I'll get something to clean us up."

When I'd taken care of the mess, I climbed back into bed and slid my arm around him. He wrapped himself around me, sleepy-kissed the side of my head, and mumbled that he loved me. It still made my heart stutter when he said those words to me.

I kissed his chest, just over his heart, and smiled. My last thought before I fell asleep was it couldn't get better than that.

———

CARTER WAS EERILY CALM before the wedding. When Will and I got out of bed, Carter was doing laps in the pool. I made coffee, Will toasted bagels, and the three of us sat on the back patio chatting. I petted Missy's forehead and snuck her bits of my bagel, and even though Carter hated when I did that, he didn't say anything.

He was just... calm. Like he'd found zen or something.

I was more nervous than him, and when the three of us walked out into the living room all suited up, I had to take a few deep breaths.

"You okay?" Carter asked.

"How can you not be nervous?" I asked.

"I'm just not," he answered with a smile. "I'm very sure about this."

I fixed his tie—not that it needed fixing, but I had to have something to do with my hands. "Well, you look very handsome. Isaac's a very lucky man."

"He is," Carter said simply. "But I'm lucky to have him too."

I hugged him. "I'm happy for you, Carter."

Carter looked at Will. "Look at the both of you," he said. "You both look great."

I walked over to Will, brushed down his jacket, and kissed him lightly on the lips. "Well, Will does."

He smiled, the eye-crinkling kind of smile, and leaned in and kissed me softly. "You look beautiful."

Carter groaned from across the room. "Okay, enough. You're making me miss Isaac." He exhaled loudly. "Can we leave now? I'd like to get there a bit early."

I grinned at him. "I'll just grab Missy."

"What for?"

"Because she's coming with us, yes?"

"Well, no, I didn't think she would."

I stared at him. "But Brady gets to go."

"That's a bit different, Mark."

"No, it's not," I replied. "She should be there, Carter."

I don't know if he argued any further, because I was already out in the sunroom grabbing her leash. I came back with her hooked up, not sure which one of us was smiling the biggest. Will grinned at me, and Carter just sighed. "You're impossible."

"And you love me," I said.

Two minutes later, we were in Will's car, Carter was in the front, giving directions and Missy and me sat in the back, on our way to Wompatuck State Park.

It was only right that they got married in the Park they went to all the time. It was a beautiful spring day; there were flowers by the pond, the birds were chirping, and a small crowd was already gathered by some rows of chairs.

I didn't know many people. I recognized a few faces from Carter's work so while Carter went off to the see the celebrant, we headed toward Rani, Kate, and Luke.

I made introductions, telling them Will was my boyfriend. It was something I didn't think I'd ever tire of saying, and while we made small talk, the crowd grew and it wasn't long before Hannah, Carlos, and Ada arrived with a very dashing-looking Isaac and a recently groomed Brady.

We took our places, and in the warm sunshine down by the pond, we watched Carter and Isaac say 'I do'.

It was a short ceremony, but no less emotional. The vows were traditional, which surprised me, but the way Isaac's voice cracked put a lump in my throat. He held onto Carter like his life depended on it, and I was only just beginning to understand how much it did.

When you loved someone—or in my case, when you

finally admit that you loved someone—and they held your heart in their hands, it is your very life you're giving them.

Will squeezed my hand, and I realized people were clapping and Hannah was crying. Carter and Isaac were facing us with their hands joined. They were finally married.

I never thought I'd be the type to cry at a wedding. And I didn't cry, per se. It must have been allergies or something. Who the hell has a wedding in the outdoors in Spring? I mean, come on.

"You okay?" Will asked quietly.

I nodded and blinked back my tears. "I'm fine. Damn allergies or something."

He nodded knowingly and rubbed my back.

People were congratulating the happy couple, so I handed Missy's lead over to Will and hugged Carter. "I'm so proud of you," I told him, whispering the words in his ear. I put my hands to his face and kissed his cheek.

Then I hugged Isaac and kissed his cheek. "Look after him."

"I will," he said. "I promise."

They had some photos taken with both dogs and then some by themselves, and after we'd taken Missy home, we met them at the reception venue.

It was a formal lunch, and the venue looked a million dollars. Carter and Isaac hadn't stopped grinning yet. They were always touching, always leaning into each other and whispering only-for-them-to-hear kinds of things.

It was adorable.

Carter stood up and, making a short speech, thanked everyone for joining them on this special day, especially those who traveled. He said he wouldn't bore us all with long speeches and wanted us to enjoy this day with them.

But then Isaac stood up. "Excuse me, husband. I have something I'd like to say."

Carter smiled but it was pretty obvious he was surprised. "Sure."

Isaac exhaled loudly. "Today's an amazing day. And if any of you doubt that, I'm going to let you in on a little secret." Isaac stood still for a moment and took another deep breath, obviously trying to rein in his emotions. "Because today's the day I married an angel."

There was a collective 'awww' from the small crowd, and Isaac shook his head. "I'm being serious. This man, my husband, saved my life. In more ways than one. He saved me. He showed me love and faith, and he believed in me."

Then Isaac did something I'd only seen him do a few times. He took off his glasses. He wiped his eyes and took another shaky breath. "I can't see. But I'll tell you this. I can see him. It took me a long time to realize, but I can see him. I can see him, what he does for me, how much he loves me, how lucky I am. I might be blind, but I can see the gift that is Carter. I am blessed, and—" He wiped his face of his tears. "—and if anyone ever tells you there's no such things as angels, you can tell them they're wrong. Because I married one."

There wasn't a dry eye in the place. Except for Carter. He was smiling at Isaac as though this was no surprise to him at all.

Isaac smiled through his tears. "I promise I will value this gift for the rest of my life."

Carter stepped up to Isaac then and took his face in both his hands. He whispered, "I love you," before kissing him softly. Then he turned to the captive audience. "Would anyone mind if I danced with my husband?"

The music started as Carter and Isaac walked to the

center of the dance floor and they danced. Apart from the music, there wasn't another sound. Everyone just watched.

When the second song started, Hannah and Carlos joined them on the dance floor and Will stood up, holding out his hand.

He led me out to where others were dancing, and he pulled me against him. "Are you okay?" he asked quietly.

"Just very happy," I answered. Emotional wreck would have been a better way to describe it. "I don't know why it took me so long—" I shrugged. "—but I get it now."

Will stopped moving and held my face. He kissed me softly and stared straight into my eyes.

He didn't have to say anything. Not a word. But I knew this would be the day we made love.

CHAPTER FIFTEEN

WE DANCED, talked, and laughed for the duration of the wedding reception, and I was filled with a nervous excitement about going back to Carter and Isaac's house. Carter and Isaac were heading off to some five-star hotel for the night, so I knew we'd be alone when we got there.

So after the newlyweds said goodbye, and as the happy crowd dispersed, we made a quiet car trip home.

Will looked nervous too, which told me he knew what was about to happen between us as well.

Walking through the front door, I pulled off my jacket and tie and threw them over the sofa. "Did you want a drink or something?" I asked, walking through the kitchen trying to act distracted.

Will followed me in. "No, thanks," he said softly. Then he stepped in front of me and ran his thumb over my jaw. "Mark?"

I could hardly breathe, let alone answer him. I swallowed thickly and managed to nod.

His lips teased mine, barely touching me, but his eyes were dark and heavy lidded. "I want you."

My heart hammered in my chest. "I want you, too."

"Take me to bed," he whispered. "Please."

I kissed him then, holding his face to mine, and he pushed us against the kitchen bench, pressing his entire body against me. I could feel how hard he was, how turned on he was.

I moaned at the contact and warmth shot through my blood. I pulled my lips from his, trying to slow things down. "Will, bedroom," I said gruffly, and taking his hand, I led us down the hall and into our room.

Our room.

Will surprised me by walking over to the walk-in closet. He rummaged through his suitcase until he found what he was after and smiled as he put a box of condoms and a bottle of lube on the bedside table.

He walked back over to me and kissed me softly.

I started to unbutton his shirt. "Will, I want to take my time with you," I said breathily. "I want this to be perfect."

He cupped my face and made me look at him. "It will be."

"I'm nervous," I told him quietly.

"Don't be."

"I thought you might want to top..."

Will's eyes widened and he smiled. "Mark," he said gently. "You're not a bottom."

"I would do that for you," I told him honestly. "I *will* do that for you. I want to."

He smiled and closed his eyes, resting his forehead against mine. "Not tonight," he whispered. "I want you inside me."

His words sent a shiver right through me, and when I kissed him, I knew there was no stopping.

Never taking my mouth from his, I undressed him. I

undid his shirt buttons and let his shirt fall from his shoulders. I undid his suit pants and pushed him gently so he sat on the bed. I took off his shoes and socks and pulled his suit pants from his legs, leaving only his briefs on.

I undressed myself slowly, taking in his almost-naked body before me. There were no first-time jitters now, no embarrassed, awkward moments. I was completely sure about this.

When I was completely naked, I knelt on the bed and made my way up his body, trailing openmouthed kisses over his skin. Over his thighs, over the outline of his hard cock, I breathed in his scent. It was musk and spice and heady and his breath hitched as my nose ran up the length of him.

I kissed up his stomach and over his chest, pressing my lips against his throat, his jaw, and finally his lips.

I settled my weight on him, nestling between his open thighs, and our cocks pressed against each other.

It sparked an urgency, a passion, in our kiss, in our touch. His fingers dug into me as he lifted his hips into mine. "Mark, please," he said gruffly. "I can't wait any longer."

I knelt back on my haunches and leaned across to the table beside the bed. I grabbed the supplies, put them on the bed, and then pulled Will's briefs down over his hips, freeing his engorged dick.

I threw his discarded briefs somewhere and turned my attention back to Will and the way his cock lay heavy his stomach. He was easily over eight inches and thick. "Fuck, Will. You're beautiful."

Then I licked him, and he moaned.

When I took his cock into my mouth, he gripped the sheets beside us and groaned. I wanted to taste him. I wanted to feel him, hear him, drink him.

Spreading his legs even farther, I poured some lube onto my fingertips and as I took his cock into my mouth, I teased his ass.

He lifted his hips and spread his thighs. "Mark," he moaned. "Please."

So I took his cock as deeply as I could and slipped a fingertip into his hole. And then a little bit more and a little bit more, until I had two fingers inside him.

The harder I sucked him and licked his balls, the more he tried to push his ass onto my fingers. He was gripping the sheets and then he growled. "Mark, if you don't fuck me soon..."

I smiled around his cock and pulled off him, licking his slit. Then I leaned forward, resting on one hand, and kissed him deeply.

Will reached blindly for the foil wrapper and pressed it against my chest. "I'm really close," he said. "And I've waited a long time for this. Don't make me wait any more."

"I didn't mean to tease you," I told him. "I want this to be good for you."

Will slid his hand along my jaw and into my hair, pulling me in for another kiss. He whispered gruffly, "I want to come with you inside me."

Fuck.

I sat back and, tearing the foil packet open, rolled the condom over my cock. I was hard and aching. I'd been so caught up in Will's pleasure, I'd almost forgotten my own.

I leaned forward again, kissing him sweetly. He lifted his legs higher, bringing his knees up near his chest, opening himself, offering himself to me.

I pressed against his hole, and as I slowly pushed inside him, I kissed him. I teased his tongue with mine, giving him my tongue as I gave him my cock.

I slid one hand between us and wrapped my fingers around him, pumping him. His eyes widened and his head pushed back, cording his neck as he pulsed in my hand.

Will's whole body convulsed and he groaned low as he came. His ass clenched around me, and I couldn't hold back anymore. I thrust hard, once, twice, three times, giving him every inch as his orgasm rolled through him, followed by my own.

I arched into him one final time, feeling my cock empty inside him. My face was buried in his neck and his arms and legs were wrapped around me, and I rocked into him again and again, my senses obliterated, the room spinning around me.

The next thing I noticed was soft kisses down my neck and over my shoulder and Will's fingertips tracing circles on my back.

I slowly pulled out of him, then leaned back so I could look at him. His hands went straight to my face and he kissed me softly, sweetly. He stared at me with something akin to wonder in his eyes.

Resting on my elbows, I put my hands to his face, pushing his hair off his forehead so I could see him clearly. "I have never..." I started, not sure what I was trying to say. "I've never experienced anything like that. That was incredible. You're incredible."

He smiled and rolled us over, settling himself on top of me. "I love you, too." Then he looked at the clock on the bedside table. "And it's only four o'clock in the afternoon," he said with a grin. "We have a lot of time."

I leaned up and kissed him. "Wanna stay in bed for a while?" I asked. "We could make out some more, order in some dinner, and then come back to bed."

Will smiled. "That sounds perfect."

"I meant what I said before," I told him seriously. "Maybe after dinner, we could trade places..."

Will looked at me for a quiet moment. "Are you sure?"

I had to stop myself from rolling my eyes. "I know you've got a big dick, but I'm game if you are."

Will laughed, and his eyes shone as he kissed me with still-smiling lips. "Dinner first though, yes?"

"Actually, it was make out first, if I remember correctly."

Will snorted and settled his weight on me. "Just as well you're a great kisser," he joked.

I held his face and asked, "Was it everything you thought it would be?" I had to know. "Was it worth the wait?"

His smile faded and his eyes bore into mine, and he nodded. "It was more," he murmured before he kissed me deeply.

He was right. It was more. It was everything.

And later that night, when he topped me—when he made love to me—it was everything all over again.

———

WILL and I got up late and were in the kitchen having a lazy breakfast when Carter and Isaac walked in.

They startled us, and considering we were wearing only our briefs, I was rather thankful Isaac was blind.

A smiling Carter cleared his throat. "Didn't hear us come in?"

"Um, no," I said with a laugh.

"Because Mark was singing," Will said, blaming me. "Really badly. Sorry."

"Don't apologize," Carter said. Then he slid his hand

into Isaac's and told him, "They're eating pancakes in their underwear."

"I figured as much. They smell like maple syrup and sex," Isaac said with a knowing grin.

Will bit his lip and blushed, and Carter burst out laughing. "I take it the six-month drought is over?"

"Several times," I said, not even trying to hide my smile.

"I think I'll just go get dressed," Will said.

He disappeared down the hall, and I put our plates in the sink and turned around to face the newlyweds, still just wearing my briefs. "How was the first night of wedded bliss?"

"About as good as your night, apparently," Carter said.

I smiled at him, but said nothing else on the subject. "What time is your flight?"

"We fly out at five," Isaac answered. "Hannah wants to take us, if that's okay. I'm sure you'll guys will find something to do..."

"I'm sure we will," I agreed with a laugh. "Any house rules we need to know about while you're gone?"

I was certain Carter would have a list written down somewhere, of times and routines for feeding Missy and Tiddles the Evil Cat, and instructions on the pool and the alarm, but it was Isaac who answered.

"Just don't rearrange the furniture."

CHAPTER SIXTEEN

THE NEXT TWO weeks with Will were something close to perfect. It was like we were playing house, but on vacation. We didn't have to work, we didn't have schedules. It was relaxing, yet invigorating.

I'd never felt so stress-free.

We'd spend our nights making out and making love, our days taking Missy for walks, drinking coffee at a little café I'd found to be suitable, and we'd swim in the afternoons and then make dinner.

Like I said, it was perfect.

It was the second week that Will said he'd like to take a look at colleges in Boston. We were sitting at the café tables out on the sidewalk with Missy at our feet. It kind of came out of nowhere, but he just shrugged. "I really like it here. I need a change from Hartford, and I thought since you have good friends here..."

It was though he was unsure if I was interested. I took his hand and looked him in the eye. "Will, wherever you want to go, I will go too," I told him seriously. "I have nothing in Hartford but you."

"What about your mom?" he asked. "And your job?"

"My job?" I asked. "Hubbard can kiss my ass. I have enough money saved so I don't have to work for a while, and my mom? Well, she'd kick my ass if I let you move here without me."

He smiled. "That's true. She would."

"Will, I would move here with you," I said again. "We don't have to live together if you think it's too soon, or we can share an apartment, but have separate rooms, if you'd prefer. I know we haven't been together for long, but I can't imagine *at least* not being in the same city as you."

Will threw his head back and laughed. "God, Mark, what's the point?" he asked. "If we both moved here and into different places, we'd be wasting rent money. One place would be empty every night. We'd spend every night together anyway."

"True," I agreed. "So the same apartment, separate rooms?"

"Well, we can get an apartment with two bedrooms, but I'll be sleeping in your room," he said matter-of-factly.

I grinned at him. "Really?" I asked. "We're really going to do this?"

Will nodded and laughed. "I think we are." He finished his coffee. "I'll need to look around to see which colleges I like and talk semesters with the dean. I'll need to find a part-time job because if it's long term, I'll need some kind of income. So there's still some things we need to work out."

"And places to live," I added. "And I guess I should try and figure out what the hell I want to do with my life." I sighed. "My aspirations of finding some rich sugar daddy are over now, you know, considering I'm with you."

Will chuckled. "Unless you can find a sugar daddy who wants two boys."

"Hell no," I said. "No one else is touching you."

He smiled warmly, somewhat mischievously. "Just as freakin' well, too."

I sighed, excited to start looking for somewhere to live. "Did you want another coffee to go?" I asked. "We could go back to the house and start looking for somewhere to live. They have some of those muffins you like here. Want me to grab some?"

"Okay," he said with a smile.

I walked inside, placed my order with the guy behind the counter, and struck up a conversation that would change my life.

———

IT STARTED WITH A SIMPLE, "What brings you to Weymouth?"

He was an older guy, maybe late forties, and he seemed pleasant enough, so I told him, "Moving to the area."

"It's a nice spot," he said with a smile as he frothed the milk.

"What's employment like around here?" I asked, genuinely interested.

"There's always work, just depends on what you're prepared to do."

"Fair enough," I said. Then I joked and said, "You're not hiring, are you?"

He grinned. "I'm not hiring. I'm selling."

"Selling what?"

He looked around the café. "This place."

"Really?"

"Don't want to," he said with a shrug. "Divorce," he

added, as though that was explanation enough. "You know the saying about a woman scorned?"

"Yeah."

"Well, I'd reckon it was first said by a man who got divorced."

I chuckled. "Well, I'm sorry to hear that." Then I asked, "Just out of curiosity, how much are you asking for this business? Do you rent the premises, or do you own it? I think there's a lot to be said about small coffee shops. I say this to my boyfriend all the time," I said, giving a pointed to nod to Will, who was now standing, waiting outside with Missy. "The franchises and large corporations squeeze out the small guy, and with that, take the charm and personalization, the honesty, of a place like this."

The man slowly put the jug of milk he was holding on the counter and smiled at me. "Son, please tell me you're financial enough to buy me out," he said with a seriousness that excited me. "I have worked my ass off for this place for that very reason. I refused to bow to the likes of any of those large franchise types. A coffee shop is a place where customers are known by name, not a number."

"Yes," I cried. "Like Cheers. A place where everyone knows your name!"

The man laughed warmly. "Yes, like Cheers." He held out his hand. "My name is Len Salinas."

I shook his hand and smiled. "Mark Gattison."

"Well, Mark, it's a pleasure to meet you." He handed me the coffees. Appearing unsure what else he should say, he said, "Is there anything else I can get for you?"

"Yes, I'll take two of those chocolate and raspberry muffins," I said. "And full financials for the last two years, your business proposal, and anything else my accountant might think is useful."

THE NEXT WEEK was busy with college interviews for Will, looking for somewhere to live, and phone calls with my mother's accountant and lawyer.

Apparently the little café was a viable business, and yes, Len was selling up as part of a divorce settlement. He said if his ex-wife was to get half, he'd prefer to sell it at a reduced price so she got next to nothing, and he'd prefer to sell it to someone who had the same opinions of overfranchised, underpersonalized coffee magnates.

I told Will I'd found him his part-time job, with any hours he needed, with an awesome boss. He could go to school and study, then work at the café when he needed to.

It was a win-win scenario.

Actually, it was all pretty fucking perfect.

And by the time Carter and Isaac got back from their honeymoon, we'd found a place to live. It was an apartment with a short walk to the café, not too far a walk to Carter and Isaac's, and not far from the bus stop if Will wanted to bus it to school.

We'd organized movers to pack up my place and to clear out the storage unit Will had rented for his stuff. We argued a little about whose stuff went where, and he didn't really want the paintings we'd done at Oak Hill up on the wall. We argued, but the frames now took place of pride in the living room—much to Will's dismay—but all in all the whole moving process was fairly painless.

I still couldn't get enough of him. Nor he of me, apparently.

We made love every chance we got, most nights, all night. Mornings, afternoons, it didn't matter. One afternoon, we were in bed, both of us sweaty and sated, and I laughed. "Remember when you said 'once we started having sex, we wouldn't stop'?"

Will grinned. "Yeah."

"I don't ever wanna stop."

He rolled over on his side. "Do you think this is all happening too fast?"

A cold stab of dread speared me. "What?"

He smiled and put his hand to my face. "No, not *us*, silly. I mean this whole thing. Moving to Boston, you buying the café, me going to college. It all just happened within a matter of weeks."

"I don't think it was too quick," I told him honestly. "I think it was fate."

"I didn't think you believed in fate."

I kissed him. "I do now."

Will shook his head and rolled onto his back. "You're such a sap."

"I know!" I cried. "And it's all your fault. I was quite happily miserable until you came along and blindsided me with this whole love thing."

Will laughed, a deep throaty sound. "Sure it's actually love and not a stomach flu or a head cold?"

I pushed his arm. "That's not funny. I thought I was dying."

Will laughed again. "You were so clueless." Then he rolled back onto his side to face me once more and sighed. "What time are you meeting Len at the café tomorrow?"

"Eight."

Will had enrolled for the spring semester at Boston University, so we had a few weeks until he started. I was officially taking over as proprietor of the café this week, and Len had kindly offered to help train me before I just walked in as the owner without a clue. I'd consumed a ton of coffee over the years from a hundred different cafés, but I'd never worked in one.

He was going to introduce me to the staff, show me how to do the ordering, how to open the store, how to close it. And I couldn't fucking wait.

I had big plans for this café.

It was good timing that Will had a few weeks off before school started, so he could help me and learn the ropes himself.

"What are you doing tomorrow?" I asked.

"I need to finish unpacking the last of the boxes in the spare room, and then I have to call your mom," he said. "She's coming here for Christmas, you know. I told her we'd be busy with the café, but she's determined."

"She's always determined."

Will smiled. "She and Ted have booked accommodation already, so there's no getting out of it."

"I learned a long time ago not to argue with her."

He raised one disbelieving eyebrow at me. "You argue with her all the time."

"It's my job," I said. "I'm her son."

"Her second-favorite son," Will corrected me. "She loves me more."

"That's understandable," I told him. "You're very lovable."

He leaned in and smile-kissed me. Then he traced his fingers along my forehead and down my cheek. "It all kind of starts tomorrow, doesn't it?"

"What does?"

"Real life," he said softly. "The café, then school. We're going to be so busy from here on out. I've really loved having these weeks with you—no work, no responsibilities."

I leaned over and kissed him. "Yes, we'll be busy, and

there will be days when we don't see each other. But we'll make it work. Will, this is the beginning for us."

"You're so confident," he whispered. "How are you so sure?"

"When it comes to you, I have no doubt," I told him, not caring how cheesy it sounded. "You're my one true thing."

EPILOGUE

THREE YEARS LATER

"THANKS, JEN," I said to the customer who was kind enough to hold the door for me.

"No problems, Mark," she said, calling me by name.

I knew all my regular customers by name. Hell, I even knew relationship status, employment details, and kids' and pets' names of most of my customers.

I walked in, slid the boxes of baked goods onto the counter, and said a quick hello to Carter and Isaac—and Brady of course—Hannah, Carlos, toddler Ada, and new baby Max, who were sitting on the couch in the corner, sipping coffee.

It wasn't unusual to find them here on the weekend, and this Sunday was no different.

Will was behind the counter, frothing milk, and he smiled when he saw me.

Will. My absolute saving grace.

He'd gone to school and worked at the café as planned, but he found himself bored with his subjects and enjoying the work with me more and more. He finished his degree, but instead of working in the field of civil engineering, he found himself working in the café full time with me. We ran the place together.

And it was awesome.

The business had grown so much and we were so busy that last year when the shop next to the café vacated, I proposed to the landlord that the coffee shop be expanded to utilize both floor spaces.

One business plan and a fair amount of Mark Gattison charm later, it was a done deal. We increased the size of the café and the business grew with the expansion. Will and I worked side by side most days, and the majority of our customers were used to seeing us together. I swear, some people just came in to say hi or to have a laugh with us while we worked.

I'm not sure how or when it happened, but somewhere along the way, I grew up. Will and I were still going strong. We lived together, worked together, not all the time, but we spent time together every day. We were still as physical now as what we were in the beginning, and I doubted that part of us would ever wane. If anything, I wanted him more now than ever. Sure, we argued sometimes, but it was usually only when he couldn't see how right I was. Or how awesome. But usually, it was how right I was.

Sometimes, like today, I'd have the morning off and come in later in the afternoon, but this morning Will was working and he called me to run and pick up an order from the bakery. Again, not too unusual, and I really didn't think anything of it.

The café was busy. Actually, the café was packed, and Will seemed distracted, so pulling on an apron, I called out to Lori. "Can you put these in the back fridge for me, please?"

"No, leave them. I'll take care of them," Will said, and

when he cleared his throat, a hushed quiet fell over the whole room.

I looked around at the faces, who were all now watching me. I wondered what on earth was going on.

Then Will cleared his throat. "Mark, you said once that I'd blindsided you, and I'm hoping to blindside you again."

And right there, behind the counter, in front of all of our customers, Will dropped to one knee.

My stomach knotted and my heart stopped.

Will took a deep breath and smiled. "You are the love of my life. I want nothing more than to be your husband. Will you marry me?"

I couldn't even fucking speak. I looked around at the room full of expectant faces, and when I turned back to Will, back to the love of my life who was on his knees in front of me, I was barely able to nod.

The café erupted in applause and cheers. Carter and Isaac were standing, clapping the loudest. Will was on his feet and in front of everyone, he kissed me. "Yes?" he asked again.

"Yes," I said, nodding. Then I looked around the café. "Did they all know?" I asked. It might have been more a squeak than words.

Will laughed. "I've been planning it for a while," he said. "I had them all here and if you said no, I had it all planned for everyone to start singing Rick Astley's 'Never Gonna Give You Up'. They were gonna do the dance moves and everything."

I barked out a laugh, still stunned. Then I turned to our watching, grinning audience. "He really has crap taste in music."

Laughing, Will kissed me again, then he opened the first box of cakes I'd just delivered and turned it around so it faced the customers. "Cupcakes for everyone!" Will cried out.

Then I saw written on each cupcake was the word 'YES'.

I looked at Will. "Confident I'd say yes? Or is there a box of 'no' cupcakes out the back?"

Will laughed and put his arms around me. He kissed the side of my head. "Never a doubt, Mark. You're my one true thing."

The End

THE BLIND FAITH SERIES

———

———

If you enjoyed the Blind Faith Series, you might also enjoy N.R. Walker's Turning Point Series.

The following is an excerpt from book one of the series, **Point of No Return**.

Chapter One

The four of us hit the gym like we always did after a stressful day and were met by a round of applause from the other cops who were there working out. The gym itself was a main-floor space with various fitness equipment, a service desk, and some rooms off the far wall for different classes. It smelled like sweat and dirty socks. I loved it.

On the wall facing the treadmills was a row of TV screens, usually showing repeats of different sports. But not tonight. The TV screens were tuned to the five o'clock news, and all the guys there were watching the four of us standing outside the West Street headquarters.

A reporter introduced the story. *"Breaking another link in one of LA's biggest drug chains, Croatian expat Pavao Tomic was taken down in what can only be described as a successful drug heist by police."*

I waved them off, heading straight for the treadmills. I didn't need to watch it.

I'd been there.

"Detective Elliott, it must be a relief after weeks of hard work to finally have this notorious drug supplier in custody."

"Yes, it is," I heard myself answer diplomatically on-screen. *"The streets of LA are safer. The people of LA are better off with Tomic behind bars."*

What I couldn't say on air was that the slimeball deserved everything he got. With no regard for human life, types like Pavao Tomic were best left to rot in jail.

Instead, all suited up out in front of HQ, the television version of me went on to say it wasn't just me who did all the work, like the press insinuated, but a team effort.

I didn't outrank the other three men on my team. I didn't do anything they didn't do, but that wasn't how the media portrayed it. To them, I was the leader of the media-dubbed "Fab Four"— one of four detectives in the Narcotics Division who had broken crime rings right across the city. My partner, Detective Mitch Seaton, and detective partners Kurt Webber and Tony Milic made up the rest of the team who had seen a record number of criminals behind bars.

"Yeah," Mitch snorted from the treadmill beside me. "The one-man show here did it all on his own."

I rolled my eyes before looking over at the other guys. "Any time either of you three idiots want to speak up when the cameras start rolling, be my guest."

Kurt laughed. "No freakin' way! I'd rather your ugly mug be all over the news than mine."

"The general public would too," Mitch joked. He reached over and tapped the side of my face. "This pretty-boy makes all us cops look good."

Tony laughed at me, and the three of them started talking crap just like the media did. But they gave up trying to goad me when they realized I wasn't going to bite. I tuned them out and tuned into the rhythm of my feet hitting the treadmill instead.

They'd settled in to running it out on the treadmills with me when Kurt told us he couldn't stay long because he had dinner plans with his girlfriend, Rachel. "Workout first, then we hit the bar, just for a few. It's been a helluva week."

And so it had.

We'd spent months watching Tomic, waiting for the intel to pay off, nabbing him red-handed in a multi-million-dollar drug bust. It had paid off today. No one injured, no casualties, several million dollars' worth of cocaine, ice, and meth off the streets, and one more link in the crime chain behind bars.

So we did what we always did. The four of us hit the gym, then we hit the bar. They didn't drink much, and I drank even less, but we'd blow off steam in the gym then unwind in the bar, talking crap and having a laugh. It was a cops' gym and a cops' bar. I'd been a cop for ten of my twenty-eight years. Police work was all I knew.

The guys I worked with were like my family, like brothers. I knew almost everything about them, as they did with me.

Almost everything. There was one part of my life they knew nothing about.

When the other guys commented on me being the blond-haired, blue-eyed playboy of the police force, the one all the ladies wanted, I was reminded of exactly what it was they didn't know about me.

Because it wasn't the ladies I wanted at all.

That was what they didn't know about me. That was what I kept secret. Hidden. Private. Would the guys I worked with treat me differently if they knew I was gay? Maybe... probably...

I wasn't ashamed. I wasn't scared. I didn't flaunt being gay because I didn't want it to precede me. I wanted to be known for being a *good* cop, not a *gay* cop. But above all, I kept my sexuality to myself because it was no one else's goddamn business.

After twenty minutes on the treadmill, I jumped off, ready for my bag workout. Boxing was my thing. The gym had a sparring room —no ring, just mats and pads. It was mostly just a form of fitness and a little self-defense. The other guys on my team didn't bother with it. They'd watch me spar sometimes, and they'd tease and taunt me, but not one of them had the balls to spar with me.

I headed into the boxing room, and Chris, the owner of the gym, followed me. "Hey, Matt!" he called from the door. "There'll be a new trainer taking your session today."

"No worries," I replied. "Is Vinnie okay?"

"Yeah, yeah," Chris nodded. "Just a change in his work schedule, that's all." He looked over my shoulder and called some guy over. "Frankie, this here is Matthew Elliott. He's your five-thirty appointment. Matt, this is Frankie."

I looked at him then, my new boxing trainer. And I got stuck.

Jesus fucking Christ.

I did a double take, trying not to give myself away. But he was fucking beautiful. He had dark hair, dark skin, dark eyes. He was European, or Asian. Or both.

He smiled. Oh, fuck. His smile.

"Frankie's real name I can't pronounce," Chris went on to say with a laugh. "But he knows I'm an ex-cop and not overly bright, so he forgives me."

This Frankie guy extended his hand and introduced himself formally. "Kira Takeo Franco." I couldn't detect an accent, but his name rolled erotically off his tongue. I shook his hand, and our eyes met. It was like I couldn't look away. His stare deepened for just a second and his eyes flashed, as though he could tell I found him attractive. Then he smiled and said, "You're the guy on TV."

"The one and the same," Chris said. "Anyway," he continued to me with a smile, "I've seen Frankie in action and thought I'd come in and watch how he does with our best student."

Then the door behind me swung open, and Mitch, Kurt and Tony walked in.

I looked at my team standing in the door, all smiling, then back to Chris. "And what are they here for?"

Chris answered hesitantly. "Well, Frankie's pretty good. I might have told them it could be... entertaining."

I looked at the three smiling cops, my so-called partners. "And you guys have come in to watch me get my ass kicked?"

They nodded and laughed, and Mitch defended me... well, kind of. "I got twenty on ya," he said. He threw his thumb back at Kurt and Tony. "These two aren't so confident."

I rolled my eyes and smiled at them, then started strapping my hands. When I turned around and saw my sparring partner, I almost lost my breath. He was stretching out—his broad shoulders were barely concealed by his singlet top, revealing well-defined muscles and beautiful, olive skin. My dick twitched.

Goddamn it.

A hard-on in front of my team was the last thing I needed. I faced the wall, bounced on my toes, and shook it out, wishing like hell my old trainer, the very not-attractive Vinnie, was still my trainer.

"Okay, we'll start on the bag," Frankie said.

He held the punching bag still while I practiced jabs and sequences, and he grinned. His dark eyes were bright and smiling as he held the bag steady. Even though I knew he was staring straight at me, I deliberately didn't look at him and kept my eyes on the bag instead.

But then he called time and picked up hand pads. He stood ready, his covered hands up between us, waiting for me to aim practice jabs into the pads. And in front of our audience, we went through the motions. I jabbed, he deflected. But he smiled as though he was daring me.

It was as though his full lips, his almond-shaped eyes, that shiny black hair, and the dimple in his left cheek were goading me. Luring me.

And my dick twitched again.

Fuck.

"Okay, Frankie," Chris called out. "Show him what you got."

Slipping his hands out of the padded mitts and throwing them to the sidewall, Frankie turned to face me. I faced him front on, raising my hands to protect my chin as he did the same.

We danced around each other for a while offering a few jabs each, and I noticed him lifting his right foot just slightly so his heel left the mat, but not his toes.

He wasn't just a boxer. He was a kickboxer.

"Keep your foot down," I told him.

His eyebrows lifted and he smirked, making my dick twitch again. And then he jabbed me twice in the mouth.

The other guys cheered as I pulled back, resizing my opponent. "Keep your elbows in," he instructed. "And keep your hands up."

I stepped in quickly, throwing a sharp left. He dodged it easily and grinned again, but this time he chuckled. And I could feel myself getting hard.

We exchanged a few taps, skirting around each other. I landed a few good shots, as did he. But I was distracted, and he landed some rib shots and a few face shots. Not that he hit me hard, just a gentle tap to prove he *could* really hit me if he wanted.

One thing I learned real quick—getting tapped in the face and jabbed in the ribs does little for hard-ons. The more he hit me, the less turned on I got.

And just so I didn't get a fully fledged hard-on, I let him win.

I lowered my hands, just a little, and I didn't move my feet.

"Oh, come on," Mitch yelled at me. "What the hell do you think you're doing, Elliott? You can fight better than that!"

I knew I could, and I thought this Frankie guy knew it too, because not long after that, he called it quits.

Kurt and Tony crowed their victory, and Chris proudly clapped his new trainer on the shoulder. Mitch scoffed at me. "Yeah, thanks, partner. You cost me twenty bucks! It's your damn round. So get your ass to the bar and get buyin'."

I nodded, unwrapping my hands. "Yeah, yeah," I mumbled with a laugh. "Meet you there in five." I didn't even watch them leave.

Because then it was just me and him.

"Are you okay?" he asked, pulling strapping tape off his hand. "You were holding back on me."

I thought he'd picked up on that. I ignored his question. I ignored his smile and I ignored the fact we were alone. "You do martial arts?"

He nodded and smiled. "Yeah."

"I could tell," I said. "The way you lift your foot. It's a defensive move for kickboxers."

I looked at him then, and he was staring at me.

Fuck.

"Good detective work, Detective," he said with a grin. "Now why did you hold back? You don't seem the type to be intimidated by a little martial arts."

I snorted out a laugh at the likelihood of that. "I'm not intimidated."

He smirked and stepped closer to me. His eyes were so goddamn piercing, so brown they were almost black. His jet-black hair was damp and messy, and his perfect lips were smiling, just a little, in a smug kinda smirk.

Right then, I wasn't the kind of cop who could hold his own. I was a deer caught in headlights, mesmerized by this man, how beautiful he was. How close he was...

His voice was quiet. "So if you're not intimidated, are you interested? Because you look at me like you could be interested. And I have to say, I wouldn't mind."

Jesus.

I took an automatic step back from him, breaking my dazed trance, and pulled roughly at the tape on my hands. I cleared my throat. "I um... I ca—I can't." I was fucking stammering. And breathing too hard. "I have to go. They're expecting me."

Like some shit-scared little boy, I all but bolted out the door and into the showers.

Fifteen minutes later, cold-showered and somewhat clear-headed, I walked into the bar certain of two things.

If I was going to stay in my very comfortable closet, I needed to avoid my new boxing trainer.

And I needed a fucking drink.

————

You can find Point of No Return at Amazon, or more information on her website.

ABOUT THE AUTHOR

N.R. Walker is an Australian author, who loves her genre of gay romance.
She loves writing and spends far too much time doing it, but wouldn't have it any other way.

She is many things: a mother, a wife, a sister, a writer. She has pretty, pretty boys who live in her head, who don't let her sleep at night unless she gives them life with words.

She likes it when they do dirty, dirty things... but likes it even more when they fall in love.

She used to think having people in her head talking to her was weird, until one day she happened across other writers who told her it was normal.

She's been writing ever since...

————

Contact the Author
nrwalker@nrwalker.net

ALSO BY N.R. WALKER

The Spencer Cohen Series, Book Two

The Spencer Cohen Series, Book Three

The Spencer Cohen Series, Yanni's Story

Blood & Milk

The Weight Of It All

A Very Henry Christmas (The Weight of It All 1.5)

Perfect Catch

Switched

Imago

Imagines

Red Dirt Heart Imago

On Davis Row

Finders Keepers

Evolved

TITLES IN AUDIO:

Cronin's Key

Cronin's Key II

Cronin's Key III

Red Dirt Heart

Red Dirt Heart 2

Red Dirt Heart 3

Red Dirt Heart 4

The Weight Of It All

Switched

Point of No Return

Breaking Point

Spencer Cohen Book One

Spencer Cohen Book Two

FREE READS:

Sixty Five Hours

Learning to Feel

His Grandfather's Watch (And The Story of Billy and Hale)

The Twelfth of Never (Blind Faith 3.5)

Twelve Days of Christmas (Sixty Five Hours Christmas)

Best of Both Worlds

TRANSLATED TITLES:

Fiducia Cieca (Italian translation of Blind Faith)

Attraverso Questi Occhi (Italian translation of Through These Eyes)

Preso alla Sprovvista (Italian translation of Blindside)

Il giorno del Mai (Italian translation of Blind Faith 3.5)

Cuore di Terra Rossa (Italian translation of Red Dirt Heart)

Cuore di Terra Rossa 2 (Italian translation of Red Dirt Heart 2)

Cuore di Terra Rossa 3 (Italian translation of Red Dirt Heart 3)

Cuore di Terra Rossa 4 (Italian translation of Red Dirt Heart 4)

Confiance Aveugle (French translation of *Blind Faith*)

A travers ces yeux: Confiance Aveugle 2 (French translation of *Through These Eyes*)

Aveugle: Confiance Aveugle 3 (French translation of *Blindside*)

À Jamais (French translation of *Blind Faith 3.5*)

Cronin's Key (French translation)

Cronin's Key II (French translation)

Au Coeur de Sutton Station (French translation of *Red Dirt Heart*)

Partir ou rester (French translation of *Red Dirt Heart 2*)

Faire Face (French translation of *Red Dirt Heart 3*)

Trouver sa Place (French translation of *Red Dirt Heart 4*)

Rote Erde (German translation of *Red Dirt Heart*)

Rote Erde 2 (German translation of *Red Dirt Heart 2*)

CPSIA information can be obtained
at www.ICGtesting.com
Printed in the USA
BVHW081048060521
606648BV00001B/150